Rac

Frank put on spe... ... ...
brother. For a few moments, Joe disappeared from
view. Frank came to a turn and realized this was the
spot where Joe told him to take a hard left. But the
trail marker seemed to be pointing to the soft left.
Frank listened for sounds of the racers, but with all
the noise behind him, and the sound of the crowd,
it was hard to tell.

Frank had no time to make up his mind. He
followed the sign, hoping he'd done the right thing.
After he made the turn, he looked for Joe, but saw
only trouble. The trail ended a dozen yards ahead
—at a sheer cliff!

He squeezed the brakes as if his life depended on
it—which it did!

The Hardy Boys Mystery Stories

Available from MINSTREL Books

126

The HARDY BOYS®

RACING TO DISASTER

FRANKLIN W. DIXON

A
MINSTREL®
BOOK

PUBLISHED BY POCKET BOOKS

New York   London   Toronto   Sydney   Tokyo   Singapore

A MINSTREL PAPERBACK *Original*

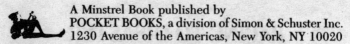

A Minstrel Book published by
POCKET BOOKS, a division of Simon & Schuster Inc.
1230 Avenue of the Americas, New York, NY 10020

Copyright © 1994 by Simon & Schuster Inc.
Front cover illustration by Vince Natale

Produced by Mega-Books of New York, Inc.

ISBN: 0-671-87210-9

First Minstrel Books printing July 1994

10 9 8 7 6 5 4 3 2 1

Contents

1 Sabotage!

"Radical!" Chet Morton shouted as his friend Joe Hardy spun his mountain bike to a stop. Dirt sprayed up around Joe's thick tires. Joe removed his neon green and yellow helmet and looked at his watch to check his time.

"Pretty good," Joe's brother Frank agreed. "Especially for an amateur."

Joe had just finished putting his bike through a trial run on the downhill course at Wolf Mountain. All around them, the place was buzzing with activity. The Hardys and their friend Chet had come to the mountains outside Los Angeles, California, for the annual Wolf Mountain Annihilator, a nationally known mountain biking race. For four days, top mountain bikers from all over the country were going to be racing against one another.

Back home in Bayport, Joe had qualified to compete for a wildcard spot in the race. Now he was getting a little nervous. The wildcard spot was his only chance to race with the pros. Otherwise, Joe would have to compete in the less important amateur races that were to take place throughout the competition. At seventeen, Joe was a natural athlete. Already an accomplished wrestler, he now hoped to conquer the sport of mountain biking.

According to his watch, Joe had raced down the practice slope with his fastest time so far.

"Two minutes and twenty seconds!" Chet confirmed, smiling broadly. "I bet even the pros don't do that well."

Around them, dozens of other amateurs were careening down Wolf Mountain. During the winter, the track was a ski slope. Now, racers in colorful outfits were charging down the hill on their bikes. Most of the morning had been pretty much a free-for-all, because the competition's organizers had allowed all the amateurs to take to the downhill slope for practice. In the afternoon, there would be an organized competition for the wildcard slots.

A racer plowed past the spot where Joe, Frank, and Chet were standing, spraying dirt behind him. Joe frowned at the thought of how stiff the competition was going to be.

2

Frank Hardy must have seen the concerned expression on his brother's face. "Don't worry, kiddo," Frank said reassuringly. "That was a super run. I know you'll qualify." At eighteen, Frank was a year older than Joe.

Joe ran his hands through his blond hair and let out a long sigh. "I have a good chance. But there have got to be a hundred guys here who all want the spot I'm going for. Not to mention Mauro Moreno," he added dejectedly. "How am I going to win against a former champion?"

Just then, the famous racer himself strode by, limping noticeably, his bike lifted up onto his shoulder. Joe noticed that Moreno looked a lot younger than twenty-seven, with his lean build, baby face, and spiky red hair. His face wore a serious look as he passed them. A short, gray-haired man hurried next to Moreno, gesturing wildly.

Moreno stopped in his tracks, gave the gray-haired man a big grin, and said, "Ease up, Don. I'm back, and I'm ready. Not even Rich Alexander is going to stop me from winning the Annihilator. So what if I have to compete for a wildcard spot?"

"But what if you don't make it?" the shorter man said, a worried look furrowing his brow. "All the money I've spent on you—"

"Will go to waste," Moreno finished for him. He smiled broadly and punched the man lightly on the arm. "And there's no way I'm going to let that happen."

With that, Moreno walked toward the ski lifts that took the racers to the top of the hill. The gray-haired man scurried after him.

"That guy sure seems full of himself," Chet said, glancing in Moreno's direction.

"He has a right to be," Joe confirmed. "Until he had a major accident three years ago, Mauro Moreno was the top-ranked mountain bicyclist. You name it—downhill, hot-rodding, cross-country—he could do it all and better than anyone."

"So what happened?" Frank asked. "What's a hotshot like him doing in the qualifying race?"

"He's been out of commission for three years," Chet said. "Did you notice his limp? After the accident, he had to do intensive physical therapy for his knee."

When Joe gave him a quizzical look, Chet went on. "On the plane out here, I read an article about him in your mountain biking magazine. While you guys napped, I was busy studying the competition!"

Joe reached over to give his friend a high five. "Thanks, buddy. What else did you learn?"

Putting a hand to his thick chin, Chet thought for a moment. "That guy with Moreno must have been Don Jackson, president of Jackson Bike Company. They're Mauro's sponsor."

"Who's Rich Alexander?" Frank asked. "The one Moreno was just talking about?"

"Alexander is the top-ranked racer this year,"

Chet explained. "Just below him is Brett Baldwin."

"Mountain biking's youngest star," Joe added. "Chet, you sure are up on your facts."

"You bet. I even read about all the new designs in bike technology." Chet looked at Joe's bright red bike. "I hate to tell you, Joe, but even though your bike is brand-new, it's already out-of-date."

Joe frowned and rolled his eyes. "Tell me about it. The way these bikes change, I was behind the times as soon as I walked out of the store!"

"What do you mean?" Frank asked. "It looks fine to me."

"Get with the program, Frank," Chet joked, pointing to the bike. "The suspension isn't hydraulic, and Joe's front brakes aren't even disc. Not to mention the fact that the bike doesn't have any back suspension at all. Joe's really going to have to race well to compete with all the high-tech stuff these professional guys use."

"Thanks, Chet," Joe said, smiling ruefully. "As if I weren't worried enough before. Now I'm terrified! Come on," he said, glancing at his watch. "Time to check in for the race!"

The downhill course was emptying as most of the competitors headed down the mountain to an office at the center of the resort's complex. During the winter, Wolf Mountain was a popular ski resort. Since it was May and the snow had melted, the resort was hosting the mountain biking competition. From the material the race's organizers

5

had sent him, Joe knew that most of the competitors were staying at condos and cabins at the resort. One of the ski slopes was being used for the downhill portions of the competition. Cross-country routes surrounding the resort were the site of other segments of the race.

Joe, Frank, and Chet had arrived early that morning after flying into Los Angeles and renting a car at the airport. Wolf Mountain was a three-hour drive north and east into the mountains. At three thousand feet, the resort area was covered in tall ponderosa pines. Steep canyons surrounded the resort, making it the perfect site for grueling cross-country and downhill competition.

As soon as they had arrived, Chet and the Hardys had checked into their cabin. Since then, Joe had been taking his practice runs on the downhill slope while the resort started to fill up with competitors.

Now, the parking area next to the resort office was jammed with cars, while racers, their parents, and their sponsors scrambled to check in, find their cabins, and prepare for the day's events. Horns were blaring, people were shouting, and bikes were everywhere.

"Come on," Joe urged. "We've got to fight this crowd to check in and find out when my qualifying heat is." He led the way through the parked cars, carrying his bike on his shoulder. Even though there were bike racks in front of the resort office, Joe decided to keep his bike with him. He didn't know if there was a problem with theft at these races, but since this was his only bike, he decided not to risk it.

The resort office was a sprawling one-story building made out of cedar and glass and built above ground on stilts—obviously in case of blizzards. Wide porches stretched around all four sides of the building. A line of people waited on the front porch to get inside the office. All the competitors had their bikes with them. Joe picked up a packet on a table that included a brochure outlining the Annihilator's rules and regulations.

"It says here that there are two wildcard spots for amateurs and that the two fastest competitors in the qualifying race will get them," Joe said. "Whew. I hope my time's good enough."

"Even if it isn't," Frank said, reading over Joe's shoulder, "you'll still get to race in the amateur events. This is a pretty intense competition. You've got the downhill qualifying heat today, then a hotdogging competition tomorrow. After that you have to race in two different cross-country events—a minirace and a major blow-out."

"You have to be good at all the different events," Chet confirmed. "That's what makes this a tough sport."

"It says here that there are set tricks you have to perform in the hotdog," Frank pointed out. "Like what?"

Joe counted on his fingers. "Wheelies, spins, turns. It's like BMX or motocross, only you're on a mogul course." From his skiing experience, Joe knew that mogul runs were regular ski slopes that had been modified to include bumps and trenches, making the run even more treacherous and difficult.

"It also says to watch out for mountain wildlife," Chet said, opening a brochure on the local wilderness areas. He read aloud a warning about keeping to the trails and not wandering off alone. "'Cougars, mountain lions, and wolves abound in the area. So be careful, and watch out for posted signs.'" Chet let out a low whistle. "I guess they don't call it Wolf Mountain for nothing."

A lanky blond-haired boy about Joe's age was coming toward them along with an older man who looked like his father and a girl dressed in torn jeans and a neon green Annihilator T-shirt.

"Look," Chet said, elbowing Joe. "Isn't that Brett Baldwin?"

"It sure is," Joe said.

As the trio walked by, Joe tried hard not to stare. "Brett Baldwin's the one to watch this year," he whispered after they'd passed. "He's a year younger than me, but he's already turned pro. That was his dad, Mike, with him. He used to race mountain bikes, too, but now he works for one of the manufacturers."

The line moved ahead several feet, and finally Joe could see the registration tables. He tapped his foot impatiently and leaned his bike against a wall nearby. Scanning the group checking in, Joe turned to his brother and said, "Don't look, but right now, at this very minute, two of the biggest rivals in mountain biking are both standing at the registration table."

"Who?" Chet asked, leaning forward anxiously. When he turned to look back at Joe, his eyes were wide with surprise. "Mauro Moreno and Rich Alexander!" he cried. "No way!"

Frank let out an exasperated sigh. "You guys. From the way you talk, these could be superstars."

"They are," came a voice behind them.

Joe turned to see a long-haired boy, dressed in a flannel shirt and cutoff shorts. The bike beside him was a beat-up old thing, but the guy was beaming enthusiastically. "This is heaven, man. If you're into bikes, this is the place to be. Mauro Moreno's my best friend, and a guy couldn't ask for a better buddy. I'm honored to know him."

"Who are you?" Chet asked eagerly.

The guy reached out to shake his hand. "Trace Heller."

"Trace the Mace?" Joe said, his mouth dropping open.

9

"The one and only," Heller replied. "Don't let my duds—or the bike—fool you."

"I won't," Joe said. "Nice to meet you." The line moved ahead a few more feet, and Joe turned back to face the front and take his place at the registration table.

"Trace the Mace?" Frank whispered.

Joe nodded. "He may look like a laid-back rock and roller, but Trace Heller is one harsh competitor. He's been moving up steadily in the standings. He's almost in Moreno and Alexander's league."

Two workers wearing Annihilator T-shirts were signing in the competitors. When Joe told one of them that he was trying out for a wildcard spot, the man grinned and rubbed his freckled nose.

"Good luck, man," he said. "It's you and about a hundred other hopefuls. Here's your registration packet. In it you'll find your official race badge and two cards with your number on them. One goes on your bike, the other on you. According to my schedule," the guy said, checking his clipboard, "you're in trial number 71, scheduled for three. Take it easy. Next!"

It was two hours until Joe's trial, so the three friends went off to find the resort restaurant and grab a bite to eat. As they ate, Joe pointed out some of the other competitors to Chet and his brother. After lunch, Chet and the Hardys took a stroll along the pit area beside the downhill course and near the judges' station.

Banners were flying all over the pit area, advertising bikes along with all kinds of parts and accessories.

"Look at all these products," Joe said in awe. "Every bike manufacturer in the world is here!"

"I told you your bike was out-of-date," Chet said. He pointed to a table set up to display the latest in bike frames. On one of them, the seat wasn't even attached to the base of the frame but floated above the bike, connected to a crossbar.

"Too weird," Joe said, examining the strange-looking bike. "But all the technology in the world won't help if you can't handle the bike or the trail."

Frank checked his watch and grabbed his brother's arm. "Come on," he said. "It's almost three. Time for Joe Hardy to show his stuff."

Twenty minutes later, Joe was sitting on a ski lift chair heading to the top of the slope, his bike balanced in front of him across the arms of the lift. Frank and Chet waited at the bottom by the finish line. A trial run was just ending, and Joe's heat was next. The downhill course followed a ski run, and Joe knew he'd have to take the turns better than any pro. He'd practiced the run enough times to know where there were rough spots and bumps in the course. It was just a matter of concentrating and focusing on the goal: a chance to race with the pros!

Another racer lined up in the gate next to Joe's.

11

The two racers would take the course together. But Joe wasn't worried about the guy next to him. Instead, he thought about the clock he knew was timing him down at the bottom of the course. Each second mattered.

A race organizer counted down. "Ready, set." He raised his starter gun. "Go!" he shouted, and the gun went off.

Joe was out of the gate in a flash. The course loomed below him, but he broke it down in his mind. First, a rough hairpin turn. Joe crouched down on his bike, steadying himself. The turn approached. Joe cut the handlebars to the left, keeping his body low. He cut out of the turn, still balanced.

"All right!" Joe cried aloud.

The first turn out of the way, Joe ignored the racer next to him and leaned way over the handlebars. A series of bone-jarring bumps came next. Joe felt every one as he sped over them, his bike rattling underneath him.

Beyond the bumps came the slalom part of the course. Joe had to negotiate his way through a series of flags, taking each one in the proper order. If he missed one or took the wrong one at the wrong time, he'd be eliminated. Putting on speed, Joe pumped his pedals with all his might. The flags approached, and Joe cut the handlebars so close that he felt the flags whip against his face as he cruised by. Along the course, the crowd cheered him on. Flying by them, Joe let their cries push him even faster.

"Go for it!" a girl shouted.

His heart pounding, Joe spied the finish line and the clock above it. Crouching even lower, he prepared himself for the last series of killer bumps he knew lay at the very end of the course.

From the clock, Joe could tell he was racing his fastest time ever. The bumps were coming up. Joe steadied himself and took a deep breath. His heart beat even faster as his bike stumbled over the bumps, making his teeth rattle. The finish line was in sight.

Joe crossed the finish line just as the clock turned to 2:25.00. Two minutes and twenty-five seconds. Frank and Chet were waiting for him, both smiling broadly. Joe spun to a stop with a spray of dirt.

"All right!" Chet cried, reaching out to give Joe a high five. "You did it!"

"Way to go," Frank said. "That's the best time so far. No way will you lose this spot."

Joe couldn't believe it. "Five seconds faster than any of my other runs. Amazing." He tried to catch his breath while the crowd cheered for his time. "Still, there are a lot of guys left who have to race," he said, panting. "Including Mauro Moreno."

"Don't worry," Frank said. "Yours is a killer time. You're going to be the one to beat now."

13

For the next several runs, Joe's time was still the best. Several racers came over to congratulate him, ask him where he'd come from, and who his trainer was.

"They think you're pro," Chet said proudly. "Maybe you've got a new career ahead of you."

Finally, it was Mauro Moreno's turn to race. Joe had been waiting for this moment since he had crossed the finish line. If Moreno beat him, Joe would have to hope that someone else didn't come along and edge him out of the other wildcard spot.

The crowd hushed as Moreno's heat began. Joe watched the champion racer take the hairpin turn, then the series of bumps that followed. As Moreno put himself through the mogul, it looked as if he was about to fall into one of the flags. But he recovered and came down the final stretch, hunkered low for the last bumps before the finish line.

"Eight seconds faster," Frank said to Joe, his voice barely a whisper. "But he still has those bumps."

"He's going to beat my time," Joe said. "There's no way he won't."

Just then, Moreno flattened out, his back wheel wobbling wildly underneath him.

"What's going on?" Chet called out. "It looks as if he's about to fall."

Joe knew Chet was right. Moreno was trying to steady his bike, but the bumps seemed to be too much for him. His rear tire was flailing in the dirt, and the racer seemed to be pedaling madly but slowing down all the while.

The crowd let out a gasp. Moreno lost precious time. But just as the clock turned to 2:20.00, the champion managed to push his bike across the finish line.

A second later, Moreno lost control all the way. Joe watched as the pedals spun frantically beneath Moreno's feet. The bike swayed precariously from side to side. Finally, the bike flew out from under him and Moreno hit the ground in a flat-out skid.

2 Pro Joe

The crowd let out a groan as Moreno tumbled to the ground, tangled up in his bike. He rolled several times and crashed to a stop beside the judge's stand.

Frank sprang into action. "Come on," he urged Joe and Chet. "Let's find out what happened."

With that, Frank led the way over to where Moreno was pulling himself up. The short, gray-haired man Frank had seen with Moreno, Don Jackson, rushed over, and several people came out from behind the judge's stand to be sure Moreno wasn't hurt. Soon, a crowd had gathered around the racer. Frank pushed his way through, with Joe and Chet close behind.

"Lucky I crossed the finish line before I crashed," Moreno was saying, a grin on his face.

There were scrapes up and down the racer's arms and legs, but his spirits didn't seem to be at all dampened by his spill.

"Very funny," Jackson said, concerned. "You could have hurt yourself just now."

"Chill out," Moreno said, taking off his helmet and running his hands through his cropped red hair. "I didn't, and that's what counts. Besides, I qualified, right? So lighten up."

Just then, Moreno's friend Trace Heller came up to him, a worried look on his face. "Man," Heller said, looking his friend up and down. "That was some spill you took."

"You bet it was," Moreno said. He started brushing the dirt off his black and green bike shorts. "In fact, I want to take a look at my bike. My guess is that the spinout didn't happen by accident."

At Moreno's words, Frank's ears picked up. He and Joe were amateur detectives, and the possibility of a new case—right here at Wolf Mountain—made him as excited as the knowledge that Joe probably would qualify to race with the pros.

"Did you hear what I just heard?" Joe asked, leaning toward his brother.

"I sure did," Frank replied as he pushed his way through the crowd. A few people stuck around to find out what happened with Moreno's bike, but the rest of the group wandered off to watch the final trials. When Frank came and

17

stood beside him, Moreno looked at him quizzically for a moment and went back to checking out his bike.

"See anything?" Frank asked.

"For a fan, you sure are nosy," Moreno said, scowling.

"Just curious," said Frank.

Trace Heller put himself between Frank and Mauro. "Give the guy some room."

"Oh, man!" Moreno shouted. "Trace, take a look at this."

While Heller leaned in to see what Moreno was pointing at, Moreno stood up, a mean look in his eyes. "That rat," he said.

Heller stood up, and Frank saw a small piece of metal in his hands. "Check this out," Heller said, motioning to Don Jackson.

"What?" Jackson asked. "What's going on?"

"Someone loosened the adjustment screw on my back derailleur," Moreno said, his face as red as his hair. "I knew I was getting a lot of slack, and I tried tightening the cable from my shifters, but it didn't work. When I felt my index shifting go, I switched to friction."

"Right," Heller said, nodding. "Did the friction go out on you, too, man?"

Frank tried to follow the technical terms. From what he could tell, there were several backups to the shifting systems.

"Totally!" Moreno's eyes narrowed. "Just as I

18

was crossing the finish line, I got so much slack in the cable that I couldn't shift at all."

"That's why he was pedaling like crazy back there," Joe whispered to Frank. "He didn't have any tension in the gears."

"It's all because of that loose screw," said Moreno. "And I bet I know who did it!"

With that, Moreno stormed off toward the judge's stand with Don Jackson right behind. As soon as he was gone, Frank took the opportunity to get a closer look at Moreno's bike.

"Hey—" Trace Heller said, trying to stop him.

"I just want to see for myself," Frank said.

Joe and Chet leaned over Frank's shoulder.

"See anything?" Joe asked.

Frank nodded. In the back derailleur, a small screw held a cable in place. Frank traced the cable to the gear shifters at the front of the bike. He saw what Moreno had been describing. The screw was loose, and there was a lot of slack on the gear cable.

"The cable must have loosened up during the ride without this screw to hold it tightly in place," Frank guessed.

"That's right," Trace said, crossing his arms over his chest. "What makes you care so much? You a racer or something?"

"Nope," said Frank. "Just a curious bystander."

At that moment, Moreno came bounding back

19

to where his bike lay, followed by Don Jackson and a tall woman dressed in khaki pants and an Annihilator T-shirt. A badge pinned to her T-shirt read Official, and Frank saw that her name was also typed on it—Julia Alvarado—along with her title—President, Mountain Bike Association.

"I see," Alvarado said, eyeing the bike. She studied the loose screw and pulled at the tension on the cable. She made a note on the clipboard she carried, then stood up and pushed her curly black hair off her forehead.

"It's not conclusive that someone tampered with this bike," she said. "Not much we can do right now. Mauro qualified for the pro races. We'll keep an eye out to make sure nothing more happens." She turned to the remaining spectators. "Let's all get back to business, okay? The excitement's over for today."

As people disbursed, talking among themselves, Jackson faced Alvarado. "What do you mean there's nothing you can do? We told you we know who did it. You should investigate that racer, at least question him! What kind of organization are you running?"

Alvarado stood up to her full six feet. "I will not be bullied, Don. I'll talk to Rich, but unless we have proof, I can't disqualify him."

"Rich Alexander?" Frank put in. "You think he loosened this screw? Why?"

Moreno raised an eyebrow. "Only because I

20

caught him hanging around my bike just before my run, and when I tried to ask him what he was doing, he took off, like he was guilty or something. Doesn't that sound just a little suspicious?"

Frank shrugged and exchanged a look with Chet and Joe. "Maybe," he said. "Maybe he was just checking out your gear."

"Right," said Heller. "Fat chance."

Alvarado tapped her pencil on her clipboard. "I've told you what we can do. If you don't find that satisfactory, appeal to the board. Otherwise, good luck on your races."

With that, she walked away. Moreno shrugged and said, "What are you going to do?"

Jackson shook his head. "Nothing. Come on, let's get that bike back to your pit and fix the gears. After that we'll grab dinner. Then you are going to bed early. No late nights with your friend Trace here."

Moreno and Heller both frowned, but they started walking back to the pit area with Don Jackson following close behind.

"What do you make of all that?" Frank asked, watching them disappear.

"I think that you've got a new mystery!" Chet said, his voice raised in excitement. "I say we find Julia Alvarado, tell her you're detectives, and ask if she'll put you on the case."

Joe scowled. "You saw her just now. She was hardly willing to listen to Moreno."

"All the more reason," Chet insisted. Before Frank or Joe could object, Chet led the way over to the judge's stand. Alvarado was deep in conversation with a race official, but Chet bounded up the steps to offer the services of Frank and Joe.

As Chet spoke, Alvarado stared at him. Then she frowned and glanced at Frank and Joe, who were making their way up the steps.

"I mean it," Chet said. "They really are detectives."

"Chet," Joe said, pulling on his friend's arm. "Let's go, okay?"

But Alvarado had lifted her head questioningly. She turned to the young man she'd been talking to and said, "We'll continue this later." Then she quickly ushered Frank, Chet, and Joe to a private trailer behind the judge's stand. After they were inside, Alvarado crossed her arms and said, "Do you really think I need a detective?"

Frank rubbed his chin thoughtfully. "The screw on Moreno's derailleur could have just loosened by itself," he suggested.

"Possible," Alvarado said. "But Mauro says he checked his bike out—thoroughly—just before the race." She sighed. "He says after Alexander came along, he didn't have time to recheck the bike before his run."

"Maybe Moreno's right. Maybe Rich Alexander was tampering with his bike," Joe put in.

"The only way you'll know is if Frank and Joe

investigate for you." Chet beamed and rubbed his hands together enthusiastically. "Right?"

"True." For a moment, Alvarado hesitated. "I don't think we've got a problem. But why don't you kids keep your eyes and ears open and report to me if there's any hint of trouble?"

"We should stay undercover," Frank said, thinking fast. "Moreno already thinks I'm too nosy to be a regular fan. What if we pose as journalists for a mountain bike magazine?"

"Like *Trails?*" Chet asked in excitement. "That's the one I was reading on the plane."

"I can get you credentials," Alvarado said. "No problem." She picked up a phone on her desk.

"So it's settled," Joe said. He stood up and headed for the door. "Even if I'm eliminated, and I don't qualify to race with the pros, I'm already having a blast at Wolf Mountain!"

Ten minutes later, Frank, Joe, and Chet exited the private trailer with press passes. At the judge's stand, the results were about to be posted. Joe stood on tiptoe, arching his neck to see the official board that would post the numbers of two winning qualifiers. Finally, a number appeared.

"Mauro Moreno!" an official announced.

Then the next number appeared: 860.

Chet looked at Joe, then at the number he wore tacked to his racing jersey. "Joe!" he cried. "That's you!"

As if in confirmation, the official announced, "Joe Hardy from Bayport, New York."

Joe let out a whoop. Frank grabbed his brother and crushed him in a bear hug. "All right," he shouted. "Joe Hardy—mountain bike star. Maybe I'll interview you for *Trails* magazine." Frank pretended to hold a microphone in front of Joe's face. "Tell me, how does it feel to be a sudden sensation?"

Joe began to blush. "Cut it out. I'm just happy I get to race with the pros. And"—he lowered his voice—"just think. It gets us closer to the action, too."

"Good point," Frank said.

"I hate to break up the party," Chet said. "But isn't it time for dinner?"

Frank laughed. "Good old Chet. We can count on you to bring us all down to earth."

"And back to food," Joe added.

On the way over to the resort restaurant, several racers stopped Joe to congratulate him on qualifying for the pro races. Frank was proud of his brother and a bit in awe.

"That was a major accomplishment," Frank said as they walked through a cafeteria-style line at the restaurant. The three friends all ordered hamburgers and fries. Frank added a salad and a cola to his tray. After they'd paid the cashier, they sat down at a large, round table. Just then, Brett Baldwin passed by with the young woman they'd seen him with earlier. The racer stopped at their table and reached out a hand to congratulate Joe.

"Nice going," Brett said. "I saw your run."

"Thanks," said Joe.

"Hey, can we sit with you guys?" Brett asked. "You've got some room at your table, right?"

"Sure," Joe said, surprised.

"This is my girlfriend, Carly Springer." The young woman with Brett had curly brown hair that fell to her shoulders. Her nose was dotted with freckles and her soft brown eyes took in Frank, Joe, and Chet.

"Nice to meet you," Frank said, reaching out to shake her hand. "I'm Frank Hardy, Joe's brother, and this is our friend Chet Morton."

"My dad's in our pit fixing up my bike for the hotdogger tomorrow," Brett said, taking a bite of his pasta salad. "Are you ready with your moves?" he asked Joe.

"I think so," Joe said. He dipped a french fry in ketchup and added, "Mostly I'm just happy to be in the competition."

"You'll do fine," Carly said in encouragement. "I saw you race. You're good."

"Do you mountain bike, too?" Frank asked.

"Some," Carly replied.

Brett smiled from ear to ear. "Don't be so modest," he said. "Carly's a top-ranked racer. Unfortunately, there still aren't any women's runs at Wolf Mountain. Lucky for me, she's here as my mechanic. She really knows how to fix a bike."

Carly shoved Brett lightly. "Cut it out. You know I hate it when you brag about me."

25

Frank finished off his cola and stood up. "I could use a refill. Anyone else need anything?"

Brett shook his head no. Chet was about to answer, when Frank heard a commotion coming from the cafeteria line. He looked over just in time to see Mauro Moreno and Rich Alexander squaring off by the drink machine.

Before Frank could move, he saw Alexander shake his fist at Moreno. There was an angry expression on the racer's face. As he prepared to take a swing at Moreno, Alexander shouted, loud enough for the whole dining room to hear, "If you don't let up on me, Moreno, I'm going to mutilate you. And I mean it!"

3 An Old Rivalry Heats Up

Joe Hardy raced across the dining room. Rich still had his fist raised, and he was moving in on Moreno.

"Chill out," Moreno cried, raising his fists to defend himself. "Stay away from me, man."

Trace Heller was standing next to Moreno. "Easy, easy." He moved to hold back Moreno by the arms. "Don't do anything stupid," he said. "This slimeball isn't worth getting into trouble over."

At the word *slimeball*, Alexander took another menacing step toward Moreno. But Joe was there just in time. He moved his muscular six-foot frame between Moreno and Alexander. He wrapped his hands around Alexander's upper arms in a wrestling hold and pulled—hard.

"Ow—" Alexander turned to scowl at Joe. "What's your problem? You're hurting me."

"Just trying to keep the peace," Joe said into Alexander's ear. "You want to back off?"

The racer was breathing heavily. He squirmed in Joe's tight grip and said, "Okay, okay. Tell him to stop baiting me, and then we can both be happy."

Moreno shot Alexander an angry look. "All I asked was what you were doing around my bike earlier today. That's a pretty simple question."

Frank was on the scene by now, along with Chet, Brett, and Carly. "What's going on?" Frank asked.

Joe let his hands drop from Alexander's arms. "If you explain what you were doing around Moreno's bike," he said to Rich, "maybe you two can settle your differences."

"I wasn't doing anything," Alexander said.

"Right," Moreno scoffed.

Heller pushed back his long hair. "Quit with the lies, Rich. We know you loosened that screw on Mauro's derailleur."

"I did not!" Alexander insisted. "Sure I was checking out your bike. I just wanted to get a look at the rear suspension. So quit your accusations!" With that, Alexander stormed off.

"Geez," Heller said, rolling his eyes at Moreno. "I guess we got to him." Heller shrugged and said, "All that excitement made me work up an appetite. Come on, Mauro. Let's chow."

Moreno took a last look at Alexander's retreating back. Then he turned to Heller and smiled. "Sounds good to me." Before they left to find a table, Moreno thanked Frank and Joe. "You guys are okay after all."

"Thanks," Joe said as the two racers strode off.

Once they were all sitting down again, Joe asked, "Does Moreno have something against Alexander?"

"Does he ever," Brett said.

"Moreno used to race for Apex Bikes," Carly explained, taking a sip of her iced tea. "After his accident, Apex dropped him and signed Rich the very next day. Alexander had been his main competitor, so Moreno got pretty upset."

"Especially since it took him three full years to come back, get in shape, and find another sponsor," Brett put in.

"The question is, why would Alexander have it in for Moreno?" Frank asked. "He's at the top of the standings. Why upset his lead?"

Brett looked at Frank quizzically. "You guys seem awfully interested in all this. Why?"

Joe laughed while Frank reached into his wallet for his press pass. He showed it to Brett, whose eyes went wide.

"I'm impressed," Brett said. "Is *Trails* looking for the teen angle at Wolf Mountain?"

"Exactly," Chet said, nodding vigorously.

"In fact," Joe said, thinking fast, "maybe we could shadow you during the competition. Get the *inside* inside scoop, if you know what I mean."

Carly gave Brett a worried look. "Do you think that's a good idea?" she asked. "What if your father doesn't want people in the pit?"

Brett hesitated. "Carly's got a point. I'll ask my dad, then let you know. Even if you don't follow me, I'll answer any questions you have." Brett played with his spoon, bouncing it up and down. "Anyway, Alexander's not having the greatest year so far. There's even a rumor going around that Apex is going to drop him—in the middle of the season—unless he finishes in the top three in this race."

"So he could have loosened the screw on Moreno's derailleur just to be sure Moreno didn't qualify," Joe concluded.

"Not so fast," Frank warned, holding up a hand. "We've got to be responsible journalists, remember?"

Joe grinned. "Right. Boy, I'm seeing firsthand how cutthroat the competition is out here."

"Unfortunately it is," Brett said softly.

The dining room was starting to empty out. Heller and Moreno got up to go. As the two bikers left, Joe noticed Moreno's limp. "Is Moreno ready to race?" he asked Brett. "He's still limping."

Brett craned his neck to see, then nodded in agreement. "That limp's going to stay with him for life. He busted up his right leg so bad they had to put pins in to hold it together." Brett yawned, then reached for Carly's hand. "I'm beat. Ready to head back?" he asked her. She nodded, and the two of them got up.

"We'll walk you," Joe said.

When they got to Brett's cabin, Joe saw that the Hardys and Chet were bunking right next door to Brett, his father, and Carly. The cabins were designed like the resort office, built on stilts and made of cedar and glass. They surrounded a lake in a semicircle, and each cabin had a view out back. Through the large picture windows in front, Joe saw that the lights were on and Mr. Baldwin was inside.

Mike Baldwin came out, and Brett introduced his father to the three friends. Joe recognized the man's deeply tanned face from articles he'd read about the sport. After they'd said good night, Chet, Frank, and Joe went to their cabin.

"I didn't realize Brett's father was Mike Baldwin," Chet said as they got ready for bed. He lay sprawled across the sofa in the living room, a bag of chips at his feet. Their cabin had a living room, three bedrooms, and a kitchen that Chet had stocked with snacks and soda.

"Sure," Joe said. "That's probably how Brett got started. I think I read that Mike works for the bike manufacturer that sponsors Brett."

Frank appeared at the doorway to the living room dressed in his pajamas. He let out a long yawn. "I'm turning in," he said. "I must still be on Bayport time. It feels like three A.M."

31

"It almost is," Chet said, heaving himself up from the couch. "You going to bed?" he asked Joe.

Joe looked up absently. He'd been thinking about the hotdogger the next day, trying to plan his moves in his head. "Uh, no," he said. "I think I'll stay up for a while."

"Looks like our new pro racer has some nerves," Frank said, joking. "Don't stay up too late, or you won't be in top form tomorrow."

With that, Frank and Chet turned in, leaving Joe sitting in the living room, unable to decide what was more exciting: the possibility of a mystery or the chance to be racing with the pros.

The next day, Joe got up early and went off to find Brett right after breakfast. Frank saw the note his brother had left for him as he poured some juice for himself and Chet.

"Joe's doing some tune-ups on his bike," Frank announced to Chet, who was still in the shower. "His race is scheduled for eleven at the mogul runs. That gives us a few hours."

"Let's go by the pit area," Chet said, standing in the doorway with a towel wrapped around his waist. "I want to see what all the manufacturers are offering. There's some amazing stuff out there."

Within half an hour, Frank and Chet were strolling past the resort office, headed for the pit area just up the hill. A plot of land the size of a football field had been reserved for the participants to work on their bikes and for bike manufacturers to display the latest gear. Brightly colored signs and billboards advertised the manufacturers, accessories, bikes, and gear. The sun was shining, and most of the crowd was dressed in T-shirts and shorts. Looming above were the mountains with their deep brown canyons.

"Wow," Chet said. "Look at that. Apex Bikes has its own trailer."

Chet pointed to the end of one row, where Frank saw the distinctive Apex logo: a thick red line in the shape of a mountain peak with the word *APEX* in black letters below it.

"So does Jackson Bike Company," Frank said, indicating another trailer across the way.

As they strolled through the pit area, Frank saw that most of the major bike companies and a lot of the smaller ones had trailers set up. On one side of each trailer was a closed-off area where the racers and mechanics repaired and fine-tuned their bikes.

The trailers also served as advertising booths. Salespeople handed out brochures and free samples. By the time Chet and Frank had gotten to the end of the pit area, their hands were full of flyers for all the latest bikes and equipment.

"It's almost eleven," Frank said, checking his watch. "Let's head over to the mogul run and wait for Joe's race."

Near the top of the downhill course, there was

a hilly area where the ski resort had a mogul run. Frank knew from his own skiing experience that mogul runs were popular with skiboarders and other hotdoggers. They loved flying over the hills and performing midair turns and somersaults.

"Mountain bikers must love the bumps," said Frank as they approached the run.

Sure enough, when they got there Frank saw racers jumping over the bumps and displaying all sorts of fancy midair moves on their bikes. The run had been hosed down to make the course muddy and the race even more fun to watch. Trenches were full of water, and Frank could tell that one false move off a bump—if the racer didn't get his bike over the trench in time— would result in a wipeout in knee-deep mud.

"There's Joe!" Chet cried out. "Over there! At the beginning of the course."

To his left, Frank saw Joe preparing to take his run. "Isn't that Brett next to him?" he asked. "I recognize his father standing by."

Chet nodded. "And Carly's there, too."

"Let's find a spot to watch from," Frank said, elbowing his way to the front of the crowd.

Soon they were standing against the fence that separated the course from the spectators. "We've got a great view of the finish line from here," Frank said, pointing to his right, where there was a clock and several judges standing by.

"True, but remember: It's not about your time in this race so much as your moves." Chet indicated the officials sitting along the route. "You're judged on whether you do all your moves as well as your skill in executing them."

Just then, the starter gun went off. "There they go!" Frank cried, watching Joe take the first jump. "All right!" he shouted as Joe landed squarely after executing a midair spin.

"He's good," Chet said proudly.

Even though Joe had gotten an early lead, Brett was picking up speed. His moves seemed effortless. But Joe held his own, and the two racers were right in front of Frank and Chet—neck and neck—when Frank noticed that Brett seemed to be having trouble with his bike.

"What's wrong?" Frank asked Chet. "Brett's losing control."

"You're right," Chet agreed, a worried expression on his face.

Brett snaked ahead of Joe on a turn and flew up off a bump. His handlebars started spinning madly while his tire stayed in place.

"There's something wrong with his front end," Chet pointed out.

"There sure is," Frank said.

Brett came out of his spin at the last second, but by now he'd lost control and veered directly into Joe's path. As he fell to the ground, it was obvious that Brett couldn't make it over the trench at the base of the mound.

With an earsplitting cry, Brett landed in the muddy ditch. Frank watched Joe, who couldn't seem to take his eyes off Brett. His speed dropped and it was clear he was in danger, too.

"Look out!" Frank shouted.

But there was nothing Joe could do. He wasn't going to clear the trench. Instead, Joe was about to land in the ditch, too—right on top of Brett!

4 Midair Terror

"Nooo—" Brett cried.

Below him, Joe saw the young racer's eyes fill with terror. Brett held his arms above his head while Joe fought for control of his bike.

If Joe landed on Brett, the force would seriously injure him. At the last moment, Joe had an idea. He threw himself off his bike, hurtling the mass of metal away from him and—he hoped—away from Brett, too. Joe saw the bike fly over the ditch and felt himself falling backward, just shy of the trench.

"All right!" Joe heard Frank call out.

"Way to go," Chet cried.

With a bone-jarring thud, Joe landed on the course. In relief, he saw his bike tumble end over end off to the side of the course. He rolled over several times and came to a stop with his face in the mud.

"Are you okay?" Frank hollered.

Joe could see his brother jump over the fence and race toward him.

"I think I'm okay," Joe said as Frank helped him sit up. "That fall wasn't exactly fun, though."

"Hey, man, you saved my life." Brett Baldwin appeared, his face and clothes covered with mud. He grabbed Joe's other arm, and together he and Frank got Joe to his feet. Joe was becoming aware of the crowd, hushed and concerned, waiting to find out if Joe and Brett were okay. A race official approached them and announced that the competition would resume shortly. A woman dressed in jeans and a red Official Annihilator Official T-shirt asked Joe what had happened.

"It was my fault," Brett said. "I lost control of my bike."

"Or it lost control of you," Frank said.

"What do you mean?" the official asked, giving Frank an inquisitive look.

"From where I was standing, it looked like something went wrong with your handlebars," Frank said to Brett.

Chet rushed over, Brett's bike in hand. "Here's your answer," he said, holding out the mangled bike. "The suspension came loose."

"Why would that affect the handlebars?" Joe wanted to know.

Brett took the bike from Chet and gave them all a glum look. "It's the design," he said. "The front suspension is attached to the stem, which holds the handlebars in place." He demonstrated by pointing just above the front tire. "I felt my handlebars go *whack,* but I didn't know it was the suspension until just now. Thanks, Chet."

The race official frowned at the bike, then at Brett and Joe. "You guys both know that bad mechanics isn't grounds for a rematch."

Brett's face dropped. "But—" he protested.

"But nothing," the official said. "You can challenge the ruling. Otherwise, you'll just have to make up your points in the cross-country. Neither of you will get any points for a win, but we'll score you both for the points you accumulated until you wiped out."

"At least that's something," Joe said.

"I guess," Brett said glumly.

"Let's get these bikes out of here, okay?" the official asked. "We've got some more racing to do. And listen," she said softly. "I'm sorry about the rules. Good luck with your other races."

"Thanks," Joe said.

"I'd better get this bike over to my dad," Brett said. He picked it up and kicked at a nearby stone. "I'm also going to have to break the news about my lost points. Boy, is he going to be mad."

Joe felt sorry for the young hotshot, who seemed to be under a lot of pressure.

"He can't blame you for a problem with the

bike," Frank offered as they headed off the course.

"It was my job—and Carly's—to do the final check on the bike," Brett told him. "So in reality it's my fault if something goes wrong."

Chet and Joe exchanged a look. "Maybe the bike was sabotaged," Chet suggested.

"It's possible," Joe agreed. "We'll ask Mr. Baldwin if there's any sign that someone tampered with the suspension."

Frank led the way off the course, after Joe had stopped to pick up his bike, which had survived the ordeal still in one piece.

"If it needs any work," Brett said, watching Joe hoist the bike up over his shoulder, "we can do it in our pit."

"Thanks," said Joe. "I brought tools, but you guys are set up to do real work."

Ten minutes later, they stood in the Offroad Bikes pit area, and Mike Baldwin was examining Brett's bike. Mr. Baldwin had seriously chewed him out when he saw the bike, and Joe felt bad for his friend. Then, with a deep sigh, Mr. Baldwin had begun examining the bike for damage, muttering the whole time about his son's lost points.

"It could have been the torque," Carly offered. "Maybe it was too high. With the jumps, the suspension was put under too much stress."

"Possibly," Mr. Baldwin answered tersely.

While Carly, Brett, and his father went over the bike, Frank, Chet, and Joe stood off to one side. The tension in the Baldwin pit was high. The three friends exchanged uncomfortable glances. After a few minutes, Chet rubbed his stomach and said, "What about lunch? I heard there's going to be a picnic on the lake. With waterskiing!"

"Let's go for it," Frank said with excitement.

Both Hardys were avid water-skiers and never missed a chance to get out behind a boat. While Chet and the Hardys went ahead, Brett, Carly, and Mr. Baldwin decided to stay and work on the bike.

"Leave yours, too, Joe," Brett said. "I'll go over it for you."

"Thanks," Joe said, parking his bike against the Offroad trailer. "We'll stop by before the afternoon races. I hear Alexander's going against Heller. That should be interesting."

"I want to check it out, too," Brett said. "Come by and get me."

The Hardys and Chet strolled over to their cabin to change into their bathing suits before heading to the lake. Along the way, Frank, Joe, and Chet debated whether Brett's accident could have been another act of sabotage.

"We'll know after Mr. Baldwin finishes going over Brett's bike," Frank said. "If so, we'll have to start putting together our theories about who might be pulling these pranks."

At the lake, Joe saw that quite a few of the competitors had taken a break and come over for some burgers, hot dogs, and a little relaxation. A game of volleyball was in progress, and three speedboats jetted across the lake. Water-skiers plowed the waves behind them.

"Isn't that Alexander out there?" Chet said.

Even from a distance, Joe could spot Alexander's curly dark hair. "He's putting in some fancy moves," Joe said. "Come on. Let's find out how we get a chance."

"You go ahead," Chet told Joe and Frank. "I'm starving."

At the lakeside, two racers were waiting for a chance to ski. Finally, Frank and Joe were next in line. Alexander was still out on the lake.

"Nice moves," Joe said, watching the racer chop across the waves in even, professional arcs.

"Wait'll you see mine," came a voice at Joe's shoulder. It was Mauro Moreno, smiling, with a baseball cap perched backward on his head. "Rich Alexander is an old man. Just look at him."

"Just how old is Rich anyway?" Frank asked Joe under his breath. "Mauro makes it sound like he's a senior citizen."

Joe laughed. "Alexander's thirty. That's only three years older than Moreno and not even so old for this sport."

Don Jackson and Trace Heller had appeared at Moreno's side.

"You're not going out there, are you?" Jackson

demanded, obviously concerned. "What if you aggravate your injury?"

Moreno put a hand on Jackson's shoulder. "Don, have I ever told you that you worry too much? Besides, I challenged Alexander earlier. I told him I'd be waiting to show him up as soon as he came back in."

Soon, Alexander's boat roared back to shore, followed by the two others. Moreno immediately headed over, stopping right in front of Alexander. As the older racer got off his skis, he pretended not to notice Moreno. It wasn't until Moreno said hello that Alexander shook his wet hair and said, "Can it, Moreno. We're not friends, so don't pretend we are. But I'll tell you what. I'll do you a favor and pass this towrope over to you. Have fun!"

With that, Alexander dropped the towrope he'd been holding and strode off. Moreno shrugged his shoulders and said, "That guy obviously has a grudge against me. What can I say?"

"Nothing, I guess," said Joe. "Come on, Frank, I'll race you."

Before his brother could react, Joe was heading toward one of the boats that had cruised up to shore. He waved to the driver, slapped his feet into a slalom ski, and signaled that he was ready.

"Let's do it!" he hollered.

"Hey, Joe, wait for me," Frank Hardy shouted as Joe's boat roared into action.

Joe turned around to see Frank putting on his

ski. Mauro Moreno was already holding on to his towrope and giving his speedboat driver the go-ahead. Soon, the whole crew was plowing across the waves. Their drivers were careful not to cross paths, and the lake was big enough for all three of them.

With the spray in his face and his ski chopping the waves, Joe was in heaven. "All right!" he cried out.

To his right, Joe spotted Frank, cutting crazy eights in the water. From the other direction, Mauro Moreno's boat was coming fast toward Frank, but at the last minute the driver knew well enough to pull away. Mauro's boat raced toward shore, then cut back, giving him a nice wide curve to ski.

Joe was cruising. He was about to turn back to his own run, when he noticed that Moreno wasn't coming out of his curve. Then Joe spotted the towrope dangling in Moreno's hand.

"Help!" Moreno called.

"He's lost his line!" Joe cried, realizing what had happened. The rope must have snapped off, because Moreno wasn't connected to the boat anymore. Instead, he was speeding on his own steam—headed straight for the rocks at the side of the lake!

5 Wipeout!

Frank Hardy was closer to Moreno than Joe was. In a flash, he assessed the situation. Only he could prevent Moreno from crashing into the rocks, he realized. "Cut it," Frank yelled to his speedboat driver. "Hang a right."

The force of the move sent Frank flying left— directly into Moreno's path.

"Wipe out!" Frank called out to the racer.

But Moreno just kept flying on his ski. "I can't," he yelled as he sped toward the rocks.

Frank cut across him, veering into his path. By now, Frank was no more than fifteen feet away from Moreno.

"Don't be crazy," Frank cried. "Just fall back into the water!"

Finally, Moreno must have realized it was the

45

only thing he could do. Frank watched as the racer toppled sideways, his face showing a last grimace before he fell into the lake. A second later, Moreno came gasping up for air. "Help," he cried, flailing in the water. "I'm going to drown!"

Frank was still skidding across the lake on his ski. He realized he'd have to wipe out himself if he was going to rescue Moreno. He dropped the towrope and rocketed backward, tumbling over and over in the water, his ski flying off. Gulping for air and swallowing mouthfuls of water, Frank clawed his way to the surface. He pushed his hair away from his eyes and searched for Moreno.

Not ten feet away, the racer was flailing about, still managing to keep his head above water. Frank swam over to him, grasped Moreno firmly across his chest in a lifesaving move, and treaded water for the two of them. While Moreno sputtered and caught his breath, Frank asked, "Why didn't you just wipe out back there?"

Moreno gulped the air. "I'm a lousy swimmer," he admitted feebly. "I can dog-paddle, but that's about it."

Frank couldn't believe what he was hearing. "How'd you learn to water-ski if you can't really swim?" he asked, almost angry with the racer.

Moreno paused. "I usually wear a life vest," he finally admitted with a smile. "But I didn't want you guys to think I was a wimp."

The speedboat came to a stop with a roar of its engine. "You guys gave us all a pretty good scare," the driver said as he helped Frank and Moreno up into the boat. "What happened out there?"

"That rat Alexander!" Moreno said angrily. "He cut my towrope."

"What?" Frank asked, his eyes wide with surprise. "That's a heavy accusation to make."

"Believe me, I know," Moreno said, his expression firm. "But it's true. Check it out."

In his hand, Moreno was still holding the end of his towrope. He passed it over to Frank, who took one look and saw what Moreno was talking about. The end of the rope had been cut through halfway and then frayed where it must have broken off during Moreno's ride.

While the driver steered the boat back to shore, Frank asked Moreno about the accident. "Alexander knew you were going out after him?" Mauro nodded. "And you think he cut this rope sometime during his run, planning to have you wipe out when the rope broke?" Again, Mauro nodded yes.

"Rich Alexander would do anything to see me drop out of the Annihilator," Moreno said, his mouth set in determination. "But that's not going to happen, so he can just forget about trying."

Back on shore, a crowd had gathered, including Chet and Joe. Everyone cheered as the boat cruised to a stop. "That was a close one," Joe told Frank, checking him up and down. "Did you get hurt?"

Frank shook his head. "No. We're both okay. Meanwhile, listen to this."

Chet and Joe were quiet as Frank repeated to them Moreno's accusations about the towrope. When he was done, Joe made a face and said, "That means Alexander would have had to cut the rope part way while he was skiing."

"And without anyone noticing," Chet added.

"It's possible," Frank said. "He knew Moreno was taking a run right after him. And he did hand Moreno the towrope he was using."

"I don't buy it, though," Joe said. "But we should find Alexander and ask him a few tough questions."

"I saw him take off," Chet told them. "His heat is at two, and he went to check on his bike."

Frank looked at his watch. It was one o'clock. "It's early. We've still got time to grab a burger and head over to the pit area to see if we can find Alexander before his run. Let's go."

The three friends stopped at the barbecue area and wolfed down some hamburgers. Fifteen minutes later, they had stopped by their cabin to change and were heading back to the pit area in search of Rich Alexander. They were on their way to the Apex Bike trailer when a familiar figure emerged from a door to the Jackson Bikes trailer.

"Hey, isn't that Rich right there?" Joe asked, pointing out the tall, black-haired racer.

"It sure is!" Frank agreed.

As soon as Frank called out his name, Alexander stopped dead in his tracks. The Hardys and Chet rushed over to him.

"Hey, guys," Alexander said, looking just a little bit nervous. "What's up?"

"What were you doing inside that trailer just now?" Chet demanded. "Isn't it off-limits unless you work for Jackson Bikes?"

Alexander played with the neon blue and green goggles he was holding, then looked up at Frank. "You caught me," he said, forcing a smile. "One of the Jackson people let me in."

"What for?" Joe wanted to know.

"Just to check out the bikes, of course," Rich said.

"All the Jackson stuff is right here," Frank said, indicating the display area to their left. Bikes were up on racks, and a salesperson was sitting behind a desk full of brochures. "Why'd you have to get inside the trailer?"

Alexander held out his hands and shrugged. "I was curious, that's all." He flicked his wrist and checked his watch. "Well, gotta go. My hotdogging heat's coming up, and I want to make sure my bike is ready. See you later."

"Not so fast," said Joe. "Mauro Moreno just had a nasty accident back at the lake. Using your towrope," he emphasized.

49

Alexander seemed surprised. "What are you talking about?"

"The rope you were using was cut through, and it snapped when Mauro went out on his run," Frank said. "We were wondering what you knew about it."

"Nothing!" Alexander insisted, his mouth set in anger. "Is Moreno accusing me of cutting his rope? Great, just great. He's not going to stop until he forces me out of this competition with all his lousy accusations."

"You had been the last one to use the rope," Chet pointed out.

The racer pushed his way past Frank and gave them all a last angry look. "Sure I was," he said. "But I didn't cut it."

Alexander stormed off. Frank looked at Joe and Chet. "Even if Rich Alexander denies cutting that rope, I still say we keep a close eye on him."

"I agree," said Joe. "He's clearly got a grudge against Moreno, and he was the last one to use the rope before Mauro did."

"Let's see if Mike Baldwin's been able to figure out what happened with Brett's suspension," Chet suggested. "Then we can catch the afternoon races."

"Good idea," Frank said. "But first I want to find out what's inside this trailer that Alexander was so eager to see."

After some convincing, Frank managed to get a saleswoman to unlock the trailer and give them a look around. Inside, there were prototypes of next year's Y-factor frames, which the saleswoman explained were going to be the hot new item because of their built-in rear suspension.

"Is this what Rich Alexander wanted to see?" Frank asked. "That tall guy with curly dark hair who was in here before us?"

The saleswoman nodded and smiled. "You bet. Don doesn't want me showing the prototype to just anyone. But the guy begged me and said what a big fan he was of Jackson. So I thought, why not?"

"Thanks a lot," Frank said.

"That Y-factor frame is really exciting stuff," Joe said as they left the Jackson Bike display area.

"I bet Rich Alexander thought so, too," Frank said. "The question is, why did he look so guilty when we caught him coming out of the trailer? And why did he talk his way in when Moreno and Jackson weren't around?"

The three boys found Mike Baldwin alone in Brett's pit area. The front end of Brett's bike had been taken apart and was spread around in a million pieces.

"Hey, guys," Mr. Baldwin said, looking up from his worktable and pushing back his thick sandy blond hair. He frowned, and the crow's feet around his eyes deepened. "Got some bad news for you all. Looks like we've got a case of sabotage here."

"Wow," Chet said. "What makes you say that?"

Frank leaned over as Mike walked them all through the checks he'd done on Brett's bike. "First, I removed the suspension. With this design, the steering is totally dependent on the suspension. Look." He showed them how the front suspension was connected to the front fork and how the handlebar connectors fit into the top of the suspension.

"You get better control of the bumps this way," Baldwin explained. "Unless the suspension goes out, which it did in this case."

"I don't get it," Joe said. "Where does the sabotage come in?"

"Just getting to that," Baldwin explained. "Inside this canister"—he held up a six-inch-long tube that looked like a little shock absorber and fit inside the front suspension unit—"there's a complicated system. If it malfunctions, the whole suspension goes. When that happens, the bike can't absorb the shocks. And every single bump goes right into stress on the front end. Then, bingo! The fork comes loose and you've got a major accident."

"And you think the malfunction was a case of sabotage," Frank concluded.

Baldwin nodded. "I'm sure of it. A connecting pin was missing when I took the shock absorber apart. That doesn't happen by accident."

"Where's Brett now?" Joe asked.

52

"He and Carly went over to Julia Alvarado's office to tell her about all this," Baldwin said.

"Who had access to this bike?" Frank asked.

Baldwin threw up his hands in exasperation. "That's the problem. Offroad can't afford great security. If I leave and the salesperson isn't around, anyone can get to Brett's bikes. You could sabotage the bike while it's still locked up. You'd have to know about suspension to take this front fork apart, but there are a lot of people around here who do."

Joe frowned. Over the PA system came an announcement that the last heat of the day was about to be raced—between Heller and Alexander.

"Let's check out the race," Joe said. "We can't do anything more over here. Afterward, maybe we can confront Alexander about this sabotage. He's still our number one suspect."

Mike Baldwin looked at Joe with curiosity. "Suspect? Are you guys really journalists?"

Frank realized that Joe had come very close to busting their cover. "Well . . ."

"They're kind of like journalists," Chet said, trying to help out.

"But not really?" Baldwin insisted.

The way Frank saw it, they had two choices. Either they could lie to Mike Baldwin to protect their cover or they could tell the truth. Frank decided to trust the man. "The fact is, we're detectives," he confessed.

Baldwin's face broke out into a huge smile. "Neat. I mean, cool. You're not pulling my leg?"

"No, really," Joe said, giving Frank an apologetic look. "Julia Alvarado asked us to help find out who's committing the sabotage. But keep it to yourself, okay? It's important that we try to stay undercover."

"Exactly," Frank said with a trace of annoyance in his voice.

"Can I tell Brett?" Mike asked.

"Better not," Joe said. "He might let it slip, and then everyone will know who we are."

"No problem," Baldwin said. He pretended to close his mouth like a zipper. "My lips are sealed."

"Come on," Frank urged. "Let's catch that race."

On the way over to the mogul run, Joe apologized for revealing their cover. Chet kept trying to take the blame, too. "I made it worse," he said glumly.

But Joe wouldn't let their friend assume responsibility. "It's my fault," he said, falling to his knees in the middle of the path that led to the downhill run. "Forgive me," he said. "I'm sorry."

Frank pulled his brother to his feet and pretended to grab his neck in a chokehold. "Just don't do it again, okay?" he said in a mock angry voice. "Or else you may find you're the next victim of sabotage on Wolf Mountain!"

The race between Heller and Alexander was

under way by the time they got to the mogul run. Frank watched while the two pros duked it out. They both had terrific moves and sped over the bumps and trenches like it was nothing at all.

Heller took an early lead, but Alexander caught up and soon pushed ahead. For a while, Heller was able to press forward and almost catch up. The two racers were nearly neck and neck, with Alexander slightly in the lead and the finish line fast approaching.

Alexander was just about to cross the finish line when a loud pop echoed through the air.

"What was that?" Chet asked.

The noise sounded again. Alexander, momentarily distracted, lost control of his bike. At that moment, Heller dashed across the finish line first.

"I'm not sure," said Joe.

"I am," said Frank. There were no cars around to backfire, and he doubted someone was setting off fireworks. That left only one possibility: "It was a gunshot!"

6 Brushfire

As Trace Heller plowed through the finish line, he let out a loud yell and raised his fist in the air. "All right!" he cried. "I beat the old man!"

"Check on Alexander," Joe told his brother and Chet. "I'm going to find out what that gunshot was all about."

After the first shot, Joe thought he noticed some movement in a grove of trees that lined the hillside above the course. When the second shot came, he was sure of it. He raced across the course and scrambled up the hill on the other side.

Inside the grove of pines was a clearing. From here, Joe realized, someone could get a perfect view of the course, especially the finish line.

"Interesting," Joe said under his breath. "Very interesting."

At one side of the clearing, in a spot that gave the best view of the finish line below, Joe found at least ten footprints. Tracing the prints, he saw that whoever shot the gun had run across the clearing and down off the hill on the opposite side. He was about to trace the footprints when a bit of shiny gray metal among the brown pine needles caught his eye.

"Find anything?" a voice called out. Frank came into the clearing and stooped over beside where Joe was kneeling.

"I think so," Joe confirmed. After reaching into his back pocket for a handkerchief, he carefully lifted the metal object and held it out for Frank to see.

"A bullet," Frank said, letting out a low whistle. "This sabotage is getting serious. Do you think we've got a sniper on our hands now?"

Joe made a face and examined the bullet more carefully. "I doubt it. Look, this round isn't even charged." The bullet was a simple cylinder without the rounded tip that would have contained gunpowder.

Frank nodded in agreement. "It's just a blank. Could have been fired by a starter pistol," he said.

Joe wrapped the bullet in his handkerchief and put it in his breast pocket. "I wish we'd brought our fingerprinting kit along," he said with a scowl. Then he pointed to the footprints. "I want to see where these lead. What's happening back at the course?"

Frank stood up and said, "Alexander's demanding a rematch. He says the gunshots were interference. Everyone's waiting for the judges to rule."

"Did Alexander get hurt?" Joe wanted to know.

"Not really. It looks like he may have aggravated an old knee injury, but otherwise he seems okay." Frank grabbed his brother's arm. "Come on, let's follow these footprints."

A short while later, Frank and Joe had tracked the prints down the hill and over a rocky trail that ended in a dry ravine. The riverbed followed the side of a mountain and, finally, led them to a trail. Coming out into the sun from the mountain shade, Joe blinked and then realized they were standing at the end of the downhill course. Except for a few racers taking practice runs, the area was quiet.

"We've made almost a complete circle," Frank said. He pointed to the other side of the downhill course. "There's the mogul run. Our saboteur could have disappeared anywhere along here."

Joe nodded in agreement. "The question is, who did it and why?" He stood with his hands in his pockets. "We know it wasn't Rich Alexander.

He was racing the course when the gunshots went off."

"He might have an accomplice," Frank suggested.

"True, but why sabotage your own race? Unless you're worried you can't win it fair and square."

"A rematch doesn't guarantee a win either," Frank remarked. "Come on. Let's see how it all turned out."

Back at the mogul course, Alexander and Heller were just finishing the rematch. "Looks like Alexander walloped Heller," Joe said, looking up at the scoreboard posted over the finish line. Joe saw Rich had earned fifteen points to Heller's ten, and when he had crossed the finish line first, Alexander earned another five points.

"Twenty points," Joe said. "That puts Alexander way in the lead. After him, Moreno only has eighteen. The next closest racer is Brett, with fifteen. And he got all those points from his moves alone! Brett must be pretty stoked."

"I see one guy who's not," Frank said, pointing to an angry, red-faced Heller, who was stomping off to the judges' table.

Chet found Frank and Joe. "Did you uncover anything?" he asked.

Joe told his friend about the blank he and Frank had found. "But the footprints didn't lead us anywhere."

"Could Alexander have been responsible?"

Chet asked. He glanced over to see Rich remove the blue and green neon goggles he always wore. The racer was talking to a tall, casually dressed woman.

"Not unless he had an accomplice," Frank said, following Chet's eyes.

"Which may be possible," Joe said as Alexander and the woman headed back toward the pit. Joe noticed Alexander was walking with a pronounced limp, and the woman was looking at him with concern. "I wonder who that woman is," he said, thinking aloud.

"Let's find out," said Frank.

The three friends tailed Alexander and the woman to the Apex trailer, staying as close as they could. There, the woman spoke briefly to a saleswoman, then took out a cellular phone and punched in a number. Alexander stood by while the woman announced to the person on the other end that Rich was ahead in the standings.

"Could those have been women's footprints?" Joe whispered to his brother.

The Hardys and Chet stood near the Apex display area, trying not to be obvious about their eavesdropping. Meanwhile, Rich and the woman went inside the trailer and closed the door.

Frank rubbed his chin thoughtfully. "Only if she had large feet. Size ten at least."

Chet had wandered off to a far table. He came back excited and announced in a low voice, "The woman is named Justine Kaplan. She's with Apex Bikes, and she just arrived a few hours ago. She's the executive who's responsible for signing up racers for sponsorship."

"And making sure they win, too, is my guess," said Joe.

The saleswoman was busily shutting down the display for the day. Behind the mountains to the west, the sun was coasting toward the horizon. Joe realized his stomach was growling and checked his watch to discover it was past six.

"What a day," he said. "Did I hear someone mention dinner?"

Chet's face brightened. "There's a barbecue at the lake tonight. It starts at seven."

"That gives us an hour to shower and change." Frank furrowed his brow. "I also want to see if the resort can send the blank out in the mail to Con Riley. If we use an express service, he'll get them tomorrow or the next day at the latest."

By seven-thirty, the Hardys and Chet were sitting by the lake at a picnic table along with Mike and Brett Baldwin and Carly Springer. Dusk was falling, and the mood around the barbecue pits was happy and festive. Joe did hear Trace Heller and Mauro Moreno taunting Rich Alexander, but luckily Alexander just ignored them and it didn't turn into a brawl.

"What is it between Moreno and Alexander?" Joe wondered aloud. He could see, in the dusk,

Heller and Moreno stroll away from the table where Rich was sitting with his sponsor, Justine Kaplan, and several other racers. Rich was obviously fuming, and Justine seemed to be trying to calm him down.

Mike Baldwin put down the ear of corn he was eating and wiped his hands on a napkin. "There was always competition between the two guys. But after Mauro had his accident, Apex dropped him and picked up Rich. I don't think Moreno ever got over it. He lost out on major promotions at a time when he really needed the money. Rumor was that Alexander edged him out by convincing Apex that Moreno was washed up. Moreno made no bones about the fact that he was bitter. He was hurt, off the circuit, and broke. And Apex deserted him."

"He should hold his grudge against Apex then," Chet said. "They're the ones who dropped him."

Brett shrugged. "I guess Mauro felt he had to make it personal. Other companies had kept on injured riders, so if it's true that Alexander got Apex to drop Moreno, well, he'd have a reason to be mad. None of the Apex personnel are the same anyway. Justine wasn't working there at the time. In fact, Don Jackson used to work there, after Moreno's accident, but that was before he left the company to start Jackson Bikes."

"And that's a whole big rumor mill, too," Carly said, her brown eyes wide with amusement. "Did

Don Jackson steal precious information or not? Is Apex trying to spy on Jackson Bikes to get even or not? It's like a soap opera."

"And all this is happening on the mountain biking circuit," Joe said, shaking his head in amusement. "Who would've thought . . ." Joe let his voice trail off as he watched Rich Alexander storm over to their picnic table.

"What's this I hear about you guys being detectives?" Alexander demanded, his eyes blazing.

"Excuse me?" Frank asked.

Joe spied Mike Baldwin giving Carly a guilty look. "We're reporters," Joe insisted. "When was the last time you saw teenaged detectives?"

"I don't know," Alexander grumbled. "But if you are detectives, I think we should all know about it."

"Feeling guilty about something?" Chet asked.

"Me?" Alexander put a finger to his chest. "Not exactly. Here's a tip: If you want to get to the bottom of the sabotage at Wolf Mountain, you don't have to look any further than Mauro Moreno!"

With that, Alexander strode off. Frank and Joe let out a sigh of relief. "Where did that come from?" Joe wondered, watching Alexander retreat.

"I think it's my fault," Mike Baldwin said, a bit sheepishly.

"Would someone like to explain what's going on here?" Brett said, genuinely confused.

Joe confessed to the young racer that they were in fact detectives. "We told your father, and I guess he let it slip."

Mr. Baldwin nodded in agreement. "I was telling Carly in the pit. Sorry, guys. Rich must have overheard us as he was passing by."

"Well, there goes our cover," grumbled Frank. "Now we'll have to worry about the saboteur being on guard. He may not strike again if the word gets out that we're detectives."

"Don't worry," Joe said. "This has happened to us before. It's not going to hang us up, I just know it."

Frank, Joe, and Chet finished their dinner, and sat with the Baldwins and Carly for another hour. Soon, though, Brett was yawning uncontrollably. "I'm turning in," he said. "See you all tomorrow."

A few minutes later, Mike and Carly were ready to go back to the cabin, too, so Frank, Joe, and Chet walked with them. On the path that ran along the lake, connecting the cabins to one another, Chet pointed out a sign warning residents about mountain lions and cougars.

"They're not kidding," Chet said. "I read that you can meet up with some pretty nasty wildlife if you go off into the woods by yourself."

As they got closer to their cabin, Joe thought he smelled smoke. "I thought the barbecues were over for tonight."

"That's no barbecue," Frank said, pointing to the bushes between their cabin and Brett's. "That's a fire. And it's coming from our cabin!"

7 A Deadly Turn

"Come on!" Joe Hardy cried. "We've got to put the fire out before it spreads to the whole forest!"

Frank sprinted ahead of his brother and Chet. As he approached their cabin, the smoke grew thick and dense, and he began to cough. "Be careful!" he heard Joe cry out. "We're right behind you. Chet's getting some fire extinguishers."

Frank whipped off his shirt and started battling the flames. Sparks flew up, singeing his face and his hair. Beside him, Joe had also taken off his shirt and was swatting at the fire.

Most of the fire was contained in the space between two cabins, in a growth of sagebrush. Frank worked the part of the fire closest to the cabins to prevent it from spreading. He saw three figures on the other side, also trying to beat out the flames.

The two groups battled the fire from either side. A few minutes later, just as Frank was about to be overcome by the smoke and the heat, Chet ran up holding a fire extinguisher in each hand. He hoisted one toward Frank and gave the other to Joe.

"Where'd you find these?" Frank asked.

"At the resort office," Chet said, his face drenched in sweat. "I got someone to call the fire department, too."

Frank wiped the sweat from his forehead and turned back toward the fire, the extinguisher pointed at the flames. The blasts of foam pushed the fire deeper toward Brett, Mike, and Carly. "Use this on the other side," Frank cried out to Joe.

With the extinguishers, their job became much easier. Soon, Frank and Joe had put out the biggest flames, leaving only the smaller ones to tackle. When the last flames were nothing more than smoldering puffs of smoke, Frank stopped to take a deep breath.

"And we didn't even need the fire department," he said, wiping his face with his shirt.

"Oh, no," Frank heard Brett cry out. "My bike!"

The young racer appeared from the burned bushes beside his cabin, holding aloft the charred frame of a mountain bike. The tires were melted along with the brakes. Only the frame remained, and even that didn't look as if it could be saved.

"I rode my bike back here this afternoon, and I left it parked by the side of the cabin," Brett moaned. "Now look at it!"

"Why didn't you take it inside the cabin?" his father said angrily. "How could you be so stupid!"

"I didn't have my key with me," Brett shouted back. "And the cabin was locked."

Mr. Baldwin grabbed the bike from Brett and looked at it quickly. "This thing is shot," he announced, throwing it to the ground and turning to Brett. "You know what this means," he yelled. "With that other bike under repair and this one out of commission, you've only got one bike left to race with."

"I know," Brett said. "I know."

"You *know!*" Mike fumed. "That's all you have to say? I know? What kind of answer is that?"

Brett's face grew stormy, and Frank thought he saw tears in his eyes. "I'm sorry, okay?"

The young racer stormed off, leaving Mike with a surprised expression on his face. There was an awkward silence as Joe, Frank, Chet, and Carly stood by.

"Sorry, kids," said Mike, clearing his throat, obviously embarrassed. "But someone's got to stay on Brett if he's to remain championship material." Mr. Baldwin ran his sooty hands through his blond hair. "One bike! For both cross-country races. What if something happens to the frame? He'll be out of the Annihilator for good!"

"We can do it," Carly insisted. "I'm going to make sure he's okay."

Frank saw that Mike Baldwin was clearly torn between his son's predicament and the wrecked bike at his feet. "Go tell him you're sorry," Frank urged. "I'm sure it will mean a lot to him."

"You're right," Baldwin said. "Maybe I shouldn't have yelled at Brett, but he's got to see how important this competition is." With a last look at the burned bike, Mike Baldwin followed Carly toward their cabin.

"What a night," Chet said, surveying the charred sagebrush and the side of their cabin where the fire had burned the cedar a dark brown.

Joe had gone inside to call off the fire department. He ran from the cabin now, a sheet of paper in his hands. "Look what I found," he cried. "This fire wasn't an accident at all. Someone wants us off this case!"

Frank took the paper from Joe and read the message aloud: "'Watch it. Wolf Mountain isn't safe for detectives. This is just a warning. The real danger hasn't even started.'" Frank handed the paper to Chet and let out a low whistle. "Whoa," he said. "Whoever wrote that note sounds like he's got it in for us, that's for sure."

69

"Do you think it was Alexander?" Joe wondered aloud. "Aside from Brett and Carly and Mike, he's the only one who knows we're detectives."

"Not necessarily," Frank mused. "Other people might have overheard Mike. Maybe Alexander even believed our story. Anyway, we'll have to keep our eyes open and our ears peeled. I know one thing."

"What's that?" Chet asked.

Frank's mouth was set in determination. "We not only have a mystery to solve—we've got our backs to watch, too."

When the alarm clock rang at seven the next morning, Frank could barely get himself out of bed. They had been up into the early hours after finding the note. The boys had called a meeting with Julia Alvarado. After hearing that the fire was a deliberate act of arson, she had wanted to call the police. The Hardys finally convinced her that the publicity would be bad for the event and, more important, would alert the saboteur. She saw their point and kept them on the case, cautioning them to be careful. Alvarado even agreed to let Frank race in the mini-cross-country that day, so that he could keep a closer eye on the action. He didn't want Joe to be on the course alone—not if someone was threatening their lives.

By eight, all three friends had showered and

had eaten breakfast. Chet headed off to Brett's pit area, where he was going to help Mike and Carly get Brett's bike ready for the cross-country later that afternoon. Frank and Joe got to the trail just in time to see Heller, Alexander, and Moreno start their heat.

"Let's grab a good spot," Joe said, pushing his way through the crowd.

The mini-cross-country course wound its way through the canyons just north of the mogul run. From the top of the course, Frank could see the racers dive down a steep grade into the canyon, where there was a rough path between the towering ponderosa pines. Along the route, there were spectators urging the three racers on. Behind Heller, Alexander, and Moreno, the pack thinned out, dwindling into a few slower racers trying to keep up with the action.

"Check it out," Joe said. "Moreno's in the lead."

For a moment, Frank couldn't see the racers because they'd all disappeared into the thick woods. Soon he saw them reemerge, with Moreno, wearing a shirt with the Jackson logo, clearly in the lead. The racers were climbing back up the grade now. The course wound around the hilltop where Frank and Joe were standing and then cut back down the canyon behind them and to the right. At the end of that downhill, there was another steep climb and finally the finish line.

71

"Heller and Alexander are breathing down Moreno's back," said Frank. "Look!"

Moreno must have realized that his lead was narrowing. He pedaled harder up the hill, grimacing from the effort.

"Come on," Joe cried. He headed to the other side of the hilltop, where they'd have a view of the next stretch of the race. Frank followed his brother and got through the crowd just in time to see Heller and Alexander catch up to Moreno on the downgrade. All three vied for the lead on the narrow trail. Suddenly Alexander and Heller each peeled away, veering off the course and into the woods on either side of the trail. Moreno, with a last look behind him, sped down the course and across the finish line.

"What just happened?" Frank asked Joe, confused. "Did he push them or what?"

"I don't know," said Joe. "Let's find out."

The Hardys raced through the crowd of spectators toward the finish line. There, Heller and Alexander had just cruised up. They both got off their bikes and started screaming at each other. Moreno stepped in and tried to calm them down but only succeeded in making Alexander angrier. Finally, Julia Alvarado stepped down from the judges' table and intervened.

"What's going on?" Frank whispered to Joe.

Before Joe could answer, Julia Alvarado was standing before a microphone at the judges' table and announcing, "Richard Alexander has asked me to state that he is finishing the competition under protest. He asserts that Mauro Moreno pushed him off the course. After watching video playback of the race, the judges have determined that Trace Heller hit a rock on the course and accidentally bumped into Moreno, who then edged Alexander—by accident. The results of the race stand."

As soon as Julia had finished, Alexander scowled at Heller and Moreno and stormed off.

"He doesn't seem too happy," Frank observed.

"Them's the rules," Joe said. "We don't have time to find out more about what happened. We've got to get ready for our own race!"

Frank was slotted to race in the same heat as Joe. He'd been able to get a bike from the resort office and was already wearing biking gear he'd borrowed from Joe. He felt the black shorts were okay, but the blue neon top wasn't exactly his style. Joe had lent Frank a spare helmet and goggles, too.

The two brothers got their bikes from the rack where they'd locked them. Now, Joe led the way to the start of the course, explaining to Frank the various turns and drops on the trail.

"The only tricky part," Joe told his brother, "is the first big fork. Go down the hill and ride through the pine trees. There's a sharp left you take to come back up the mountain. A soft left leads you off the trail. Follow the sign and you'll be fine."

The announcement came for the racers to line up and prepare to start. Frank felt butterflies starting to bump around in his stomach, but he reminded himself that all he had to do was keep up with Joe. And keep an eye out for the saboteur.

"Ready?" Joe asked, adjusting his goggles over his eyes.

Frank nodded. "I think so."

"Let's do it."

Joe cruised over to the starting line, where the other racers had already begun to take their positions. Frank crammed into a spot next to Joe. Before he could even feel nervous, the starting gun went off.

"All right!" the racer to Frank's right shouted.

"Go for it!" another one cried.

The pack began to move around Frank, jockeying for position. He squeezed between two racers and managed to keep Joe in view. They all started down the hill, and Frank felt the excitement build. He was competing in a championship bike race!

Joe wasn't in the lead, but he was in the first pack. A gap widened between the front racers and the pack that was riding with Frank. Joe fell back to the rear of the lead pack, unable to keep up the pace. Frank was holding his own at the front of his group.

Below him, the lead racers dropped out of sight as the course wound through the ponderosas. Frank kept his eye on the trail and the markers, careful to follow the signs. Still in the front of his pack, Frank put on speed, hoping to catch up with his brother.

For a few moments, Joe disappeared from view. Frank came to a turn and realized this was the spot where Joe had told him to take a hard left. But the trail marker seemed to be pointing to the soft left. Frank listened for sounds of the racers, but with all the noise behind him and the sound of the crowd, it was hard to tell.

Frank had no time to make up his mind. He followed the sign, hoping he'd done the right thing. After he made the turn, he looked for Joe and the other racers, but the trail seemed empty.

Then Frank saw something that made his stomach do a somersault. The trail ended a dozen yards ahead—at a sheer cliff!

8 Tracking the Saboteur

"Whoa!" Frank cried out. He wrapped his fingers around the brakes and squeezed as if his life depended upon it—which it did!

The trail dead-ended in a clearing. Just beyond was the edge of the mountain. Frank felt his tires searching for a grip. He was close enough to the cliff to see that the fall would kill him.

"Eyahh!" he yelled. He gripped the brakes so hard he thought his fingers would fall off. The bike went into a skid and he struggled to keep it upright beneath him. Finally, his heart pounding, he felt the bike right itself and come to a stop. When his feet were back on solid ground, his hands started shaking, and he tried not to think about how close he'd come to a disastrous end. Instead, he turned the bike around as quickly as possible.

Just then several other racers barreled down the trail, nearly crashing into him.

"Stop," Frank cried, waving his hands. "It's a dead end!"

Two competitors plowed off the trail, narrowly avoiding Frank and the cliff. Another rider managed to brake in time, but the rider behind him crashed into the first one. They both went flying.

"What happened?" one of the racers asked Frank, removing his goggles.

"I'm not sure," said Frank. "But I'm going to find out." He got back on his bike and barreled back down the trail to where he'd taken the wrong turn. Just as he got there, Frank saw a lone figure with his hands on the trail marker, a bike nearby.

"Hey!" Frank called out. "What are you doing?"

The racer spotted Frank and hopped back on his bike, but not before Frank got a good enough look at him to realize the guy had dark curly hair. And he was wearing Rich Alexander's trademark neon blue and green goggles! Even though his helmet didn't have the distinctive Apex logo, Frank was sure—from the build and the hair— that the racer was Alexander.

"Hold it right there!" Frank shouted.

But Alexander wasn't sticking around to answer any questions. He tore off through the woods to the left, leaving Frank in the dust.

"You're not getting away this easily," Frank said through gritted teeth.

Alexander had gone off trail, and Frank struggled to keep up with him as Alexander led him deeper into the woods. Pine branches slapped at his face, the forest bumped beneath him. Up ahead, Alexander, a much better rider, was getting farther and farther away.

Finally, after a steep descent, Frank came to a ravine. "How on earth?" he wondered aloud. There didn't seem to be any way to cross the fast-moving water except to carry the bike on his shoulders and wade through.

Frank hoisted his bike on his shoulder and stepped into the river. The shock of cold water made him cringe. Soon he was up to his waist, but he pressed on. The moment he was on the other side of the ravine, Frank hopped back on his bike and started to climb up the other side.

But all his efforts came to nothing. By the time he got to the top of the grade, Alexander had disappeared from sight. Frank listened carefully for a sign of the racer, but the woods were silent except for some hawks flying high above the pines.

"Rats!" Frank said, scowling.

Twenty minutes later, he was back on the cross-country trail, cruising toward the finish line. Joe was waiting, concerned. "What happened to you?" he asked as Frank dismounted and removed his goggles.

"Alexander shifted the trail marker," Frank said, trying to get his breath. Now, soaked through and angry, he scanned the crowd for a sign of Alexander. "Have you seen him?" he asked Joe.

"Not since his race," said Joe. "The other racers told me about the marker. Where'd you go?"

"I followed him into the woods," Frank said. "But I lost him. The guy's too good."

"He's not going anywhere," Joe assured his brother. "When we find him, he's got some serious questions to answer."

All around them, Frank saw the spectators talking among themselves, sharing information. Apparently everyone now knew that a marker had been moved. A moment later, Julia Alvarado came over. Her dark hair was falling from its ponytail, and her face was flushed.

"Are you okay?" she asked Frank. "I heard you were the first one to go off the trail."

Frank assured her that he was fine. "But we need to talk to you—in private." The Hardys and Alvarado quickly walked away from the crowd.

"Rich Alexander is a prime suspect," Frank told Alvarado when they were in a more quiet area. The woman's brown eyes widened. She listened carefully while Frank told her about seeing Alexander at the trail marker and following him into the woods.

"I'm very surprised," Alvarado said. "But I'm sure you two know what you're doing. We're rerunning the race at five. I know the competition isn't your main concern, but you may as well race in the rematch."

"Thanks," said Joe, brightening.

"Meanwhile, both of you be careful." Alvarado took a deep breath. "It seems to me that whoever messed up that marker wants to see you hurt. Especially after that fire last night. I'm going to question Alexander directly, but even if he's behind all this, he'll probably deny it. So, you two keep doing whatever you can to catch him."

Alvarado gave the Hardys a last concerned smile and walked off toward the judges' table. Joe turned to his brother and said, "So, did all that racing make you work up an appetite?"

Frank shot Joe a quizzical look. "Do you really think I've had time to worry about food?"

"Nope. But we can head back to the dining hall and see about finding Alexander at the same time." He got on his bike and started pedaling. "One macaroni and cheese and a suspect—to go."

In the resort dining room, Justine Kaplan was having lunch with Mauro Moreno. "That's weird," said Frank, as he and Joe passed their table. "I wonder what they have to talk about."

"Business, I guess," Joe said. "Maybe Moreno's trying to turn her against Alexander. It sure wouldn't be hard if Kaplan knew about Rich's latest trick."

"Or maybe she's scouting out a new racer to sponsor," Frank suggested. "Remember those rumors about Apex thinking about dropping Alexander."

The Hardys took a seat beside Chet, who was bursting with gossip he'd heard hanging out with Brett, Mike, and Carly. Frank only half listened; mostly his mind was on finding Alexander. They'd stopped by the Apex trailer as well as Rich's cabin, but the racer wasn't at either spot. No one seemed to know where to find him either. Frank just hoped Rich wasn't out on the course, planning yet another dangerous act of sabotage.

"We've got to stop this guy!" Frank said, thinking aloud.

"Who?" Chet wanted to know.

"Rich Alexander."

"Funny," said Chet, raising his eyebrows. "We were just talking about him. Brett was telling me that the rumor on the circuit is that Justine Kaplan's got Rich spying for her."

"What?" Frank gave Chet a confused look. "You'd better spell that one out."

81

Bit by bit, Chet caught Joe and Frank up on their conversation, and finally Frank understood what Chet was talking about. "So Rich Alexander has been spying on Jackson Bikes just to make sure that Justine doesn't drop her sponsorship?" Frank asked.

Joe nodded. "Sounds right to me," he said.

Frank thought for a minute. "That would explain why we saw him coming out of the Jackson trailer," he agreed.

"And why he wouldn't explain what he was doing there," Joe added.

"And why he's committing the sabotage, too!" Chet practically shouted.

"Shhh!" Frank looked around them to be sure no one had overheard. Racers at the tables on either side of them were leaning over their plates, obviously thinking more about their food than any conversation. "How'd you reach that conclusion?"

"Think about it," Chet said. "If Rich is afraid that Apex is going to drop him, he'll do anything to win. Including committing an act of sabotage. He wants to make sure no one else comes out on top, so he's wrecking all the races he's not in."

Frank mulled over Chet's theory. "It makes sense." He bit his lower lip, then took a sip of his iced tea. "Maybe Kaplan's lunch with Moreno isn't innocent after all," he said, glancing in their direction. Mauro was getting up from the table, smiling and shaking Justine's hand. "Maybe Justine really is going to drop Rich, and she's looking at other racers to sponsor."

"Good thing Rich isn't here to see this," Joe said, following Moreno with his eyes as the racer left the dining room. "He'd really blow steam."

"Come on," said Frank. "I'll bet Justine Kaplan can answer some of our questions."

The executive looked at Frank, Joe, and Chet with curiosity as they approached her table. She blinked several times, then agreed to answer their questions. "Since you are journalists after all," she said, smiling and pushing back her hair. "Shoot."

Frank took out a pad from his shirt pocket. "First, we'd like to know what you and Mauro Moreno were discussing just now."

Kaplan raised an eyebrow. "Why, no. That's personal."

"Did you call the meeting?" Joe pressed.

"No," Kaplan replied. "He did." Her eyes moved from Frank to Joe to Chet. "You boys play hardball, huh?"

With a shrug Frank said, "Our magazine pays us to ask questions, so we do." He poised his pen and said, "There's a rumor going around that Apex is going to drop Rich Alexander. True or false?"

"False," Kaplan replied firmly.

"What happened between you and Don Jackson?" Chet asked. "Why the bad blood? Did he really steal company secrets before going out on his own?"

"Whoa—" Kaplan leaned back in her chair and held her hands out. "Slow down. I don't discuss Don Jackson or our previous business relationship. He went his way, I went mine. Period. Now if you'll excuse me . . ." She stood up, buttoning her blazer. "Good luck with your article. But let me give you some advice. There may be a lot of rumors, but that's all they are. Including the ones about spying." She winked and shot them a smile. "So don't even ask me about that. Take it easy!"

As Kaplan walked out of the dining room, Frank shut his notebook in frustration. "Well, she sure didn't help. I just wish we knew where Alexander was."

"Too bad we don't have time to look," said Joe. "Brett's heat starts in twenty minutes, and I told him I'd be there to watch."

"You guys go," said Frank. "I want to track down Alexander before anything more happens."

"Okay," Joe nodded. "But stop by Brett's pit area with us and say hello."

Frank stood up and pushed in his chair. "Sure. I can apologize for not being able to see him race."

Chet led them back to Brett's pit. Along the way, Frank kept his eyes peeled for Rich Alexander, but the racer was nowhere in sight. As they came to the Offroad Bikes display, Frank saw that Mike Baldwin's face was bright red with anger, and the man was gesturing angrily at Brett.

"I wonder what's going on," Chet said.

"What's the matter?" Joe asked when they got close enough.

"You know Brett had one last bike that was in working order," Mike Baldwin stated flatly, giving Brett an exasperated look.

"So?" Joe asked. "Did something happen?"

"You bet something happened." Mike took a breath, and his mouth set in a grim expression. "Someone's stolen it."

9 Tough Brake

"I can't believe that!" Joe said. "You sure do have the worst luck. What other racer could say that one of their bikes was sabotaged, another was burned, and the last one was stolen?"

"No one," Brett said. He shot his father a worried look. "Maybe we can borrow a bike?"

Carly nodded emphatically. "Sure. Sure we can." She gestured to the pit area next door. "Giant Bikes might lend us one of theirs, or maybe we could use one of Kelly's over there."

Mike Baldwin shook his head and scowled. "Brett can't race on another company's bike," he said. "Offroad could drop him. He knows that."

Brett kicked at the dirt and bit on his lower lip. "Look, I messed up. I'm sorry. Maybe if you let up on me a bit."

Joe had an idea. "Why can't Brett use my bike? We'll black out the name, and if someone asks, he just borrowed it from a friend. Won't that work?"

Brett looked surprised. "I can't do that. I mean, you need your bike. Besides, what if something happens? With my luck . . ." Brett hung his head, shaking it slowly. "I won't do it."

"What are you talking about?" Mike Baldwin asked, taking Brett by the shoulders. "If you don't borrow his bike, you can't race. If you can't race, there's no way you'll win. You're in the top three, Brett. Don't blow it. This is what we've been working for all this time!"

Brett shrugged off his father's grip. "What if it's not?" he demanded hotly. "What if this is what you want, not what I want?"

With that, Brett stormed off toward a nearby refreshment stand. Carly raced after him. Joe watched as she caught up with Brett, then tried to calm him down.

Once again Frank, Chet, and Joe found themselves in the middle of a Baldwin family blowup. Finally, Frank hopped on his bike and said, "I hate to run off, but I really want to hunt down Alexander. I'll meet up with you guys back at the cross-country trail, okay?"

Joe nodded in agreement. After Frank had gone, he turned to Mike Baldwin. "We should report this theft to the race officials."

"You're right." Mike looked over at Brett, who was still standing at the refreshment stand. "I'll do that. Meanwhile, set up your bike in the rack," he added hopefully. "Brett may change his mind."

"No problem," said Joe, rolling his bike into the pit. "Chet and I will start going over it."

As soon as Baldwin left, Carly and Brett came back to the pit. Joe told Brett his father had gone off to report the theft. Then he asked, "How'd it happen anyway?"

"Carly was working here all alone," Brett explained. "Some guy in a ski mask jumped the barrier there"—Brett pointed to a low railing that kept spectators out of the pit—"pushed her down, and grabbed my bike. She never saw what hit her."

Carly swallowed and nodded. "I tried to chase the guy, but he got on the bike and disappeared."

"Could anyone here identify him?" Joe asked.

"Nope," said Carly. "People are way too busy with their own thing."

Joe looked around and realized that Carly was right. On either side of the Offroad pit, mechanics were engrossed in their work on their bikes. The spectators were concerned primarily with the displays and probably wouldn't have noticed a guy on a bike—even if he were wearing a mask.

"You guys stay here," Joe said. "I'm going to ask around, see if anybody saw him."

Joe left Brett, Carly, and Chet in the pit area. He hoped that Brett would change his mind and borrow the bike. Quickly, Joe made a tour of the pit area, asking mechanics and spectators if they'd seen a person in a mask on a bike. After about fifteen minutes, he didn't have a single lead. Every person he asked just shook his or her head and said no.

"Rats," said Joe, heading back to Offroad Bikes. "I hate dead ends."

"No luck?" Chet asked when he saw Joe's crestfallen face.

"Not a single clue." Brett was kneeling before the bike, adjusting the chain on the derailleur. "Changed your mind?" Joe asked the racer.

Brett looked up at Joe with a reluctant smile. "Carly and I talked about it. We've come this far. We can't back out just because of a little trouble, can we? Besides, if I quit, my dad will probably stop speaking to me forever."

Joe realized that the pressure to please his father was probably what changed Brett's mind. Brett didn't seem very excited, even after Carly had fixed up the bike and handed it over to him for a test-drive. Just as Brett was hopping onto the bike, Mike Baldwin returned, surprised to see his son up on the bike. He was clearly happy that Brett had changed his mind but also seemed to be doing his best not to show it too much. Joe guessed that Mike had decided to back off on the pressure.

"He'll be fine," Joe reassured Brett's father as the racer rode through the pit area.

89

"I know," said Mike. "But sometimes I wonder if Brett isn't right."

"What do you mean?" Chet asked.

"If all this isn't for me and not for him," Mike confessed. There was an awkward moment when Carly stared at Brett's father, but it quickly passed as Brett rode back.

"All set," said Brett. "I'll meet you guys over at the course."

By the time Joe, Chet, Mike, and Carly got to the mini-cross-country course, Frank was already waiting for them. "Any news on Alexander?" Joe asked his brother.

Frank shook his head. "A parking attendant saw him leaving the resort right after the race. Who knows what he's up to? He was on his bike, so maybe he's just doing some training for tomorrow."

Joe scowled. "I doubt it. But until he comes back and we can confront him, there's not much we can do. Let's watch the race."

The competitors were lining up at the start. Mike and Carly had edged their way to the front of the crowd. Chet, Frank, and Joe went to stand beside Carly and Mr. Baldwin. Brett noticed them all and gave the group a thumbs-up sign. Then he placed the goggles on his head, adjusted his helmet, and rested his fingers on the handlebars, all set to go.

A race official held up a starter gun. "Ready. On your marks. Get set. Go!"

The gun went off, and the racers zoomed out of their starting positions.

"Go, Brett!" Chet cried.

"Do it!" Carly shouted.

Mike, Frank, and Joe joined in the cheers. All around them, spectators were calling out for their favorite racers. It was a tough heat, but Brett quickly took the lead. Mike started whooping it up.

"That's my son!" he shouted. "Way to go, Brett!"

As Brett disappeared into the woods, Carly moved toward the other side of the hill. Joe, Chet, Frank, and Mike followed her. From here, they would have a great view of Brett as he came back up the hill. When he did, he was well ahead of the pack.

"He's still in the lead!" Joe cried.

"Is that the same bike you raced on?" Frank teased. "It sure looks different."

Joe elbowed his brother. "Thanks a lot. What are you trying to say? That I could have won on that bike?"

Frank just smiled. "Oh, no, that wasn't what I meant at all."

"Watch the race, Frank," said Joe. "Maybe you'll get some pointers."

Brett had climbed the hill to their left and was pounding down the steep grade to the right. Carly raced down the hill to be able to watch from the finish line. Everyone followed, getting there just in time to see Brett coasting through the last set of turns.

"He's going to win!" Mike cried.

Just before the finish line, the grade got even steeper. By now, Brett and the other racers were blitzing. Joe remembered this was the toughest part of the course—trying to keep control of the bike at such high speed. Brett was doing a great job when suddenly his bike went out of control.

"What's wrong?" Frank asked.

"I don't know!" Joe shot back, watching Brett careen down the slope, his face a mask of terror.

"It's his brakes," Mike Baldwin cried. "He can't stop!"

10 Some Local Wildlife

Sure enough, Brett was out of control. "Help!" he cried as he plummeted down the course. "No brakes! Help!"

"We've got to do something," Carly gasped.

The crowd watched in horror as Brett hurtled toward them, unable to stop his bike.

"Cross the finish line," Mike cried, cupping his hands around his mouth. "Win the race, and worry about stopping later."

Brett barreled across the finish line with a record time. But Frank's stomach flip-flopped when he saw Brett's next move.

"He's wiping out!" Joe cried.

Brett let himself fall. His bike went out under him, taking him into a tumble. For what seemed like minutes, Frank and the rest of the crowd watched Brett somersault through the air, then land and roll down the hill—over and over and over again, tangled up in his bike.

"Oh, no!" Carly cried. She was the first one out of the crowd, racing toward Brett. Frank quickly followed, with Mike, Joe, and Chet at his heels. When they got to Brett, he was lying unconscious on the ground, covered in dirt and pine needles. Carly kneeled beside him, calling out his name. Frank saw Brett's eyelids flutter slightly beneath his goggles.

"He's okay," Frank said, trying to reassure Carly. "Look, he's coming around."

"Brett," Mike called out, leaning over his son. "Brett, can you hear me?"

The young racer opened his eyes and stared up at his father. "What happened?" he asked weakly.

"You won," Mike said. "You had an accident, but you won."

"Can you sit up?" Joe asked, taking hold of Brett's arm.

"I think so." Brett held his hands to his head. "I've got a wicked headache though."

"Be careful," Carly urged. She put Brett's arm over her shoulder, and on the count of three they all helped Brett to his feet. The racer stumbled a bit, but eventually he was steady.

A small crowd had gathered to see if Brett was

okay. When he was steady on his feet, they gave a cheer and slowly started to wander off.

"You need to see a doctor," Mike said to his son, obviously concerned. "What if you have a concussion? We can't have you go out of commission in the cross-country tomorrow."

"I'm fine," Brett told him, shrugging off his father's arm and looking away. "Don't worry about your precious race."

Now that Brett was on his feet, Frank noticed, he was returning to his normal self and that included snapping at his father. "Somebody tell me what happened to my bike," Brett demanded now. "Was it more sabotage? I remember going real fast, trying to brake, and not getting any response."

Carly walked over to the spot where the bike lay, mangled and bent. She came back with it and said, "There's no brake action here at all."

"That's what I thought," Brett said. His mouth turned down in a deep frown, and he blinked his eyes several times. Frank was sure the young racer was about to cry. "Why is someone after me?" Brett wailed. "Why are they doing this to me?"

"It'll be okay," Frank said, trying to reassure him.

"We'll find the guy," Mike stated firmly. "That's not what counts. What's most important is that you keep going. You're in the lead now, Brett."

"Who cares?" Brett pounded his fist against his leg. "What does it matter if I'm getting into accidents like this one? I could have been—"

"Don't say it," Mike urged. He reached for Brett, who pulled away.

"Don't." Brett gave his father an angry look. "You don't care about me. All you care about are these stupid races and sponsorship and my standings. Do you ever think about my feelings? That maybe I can't handle all this pressure? That I could have been hurt just now?"

"I have," Mike said. "You know I have."

"Right." Brett scowled. "Well, not enough. I quit!" He threw the bike to the ground and kicked at it. "Hear that? I quit. I've had it. That's it, no more. *Hasta la vista!*"

Before anyone could stop him, Brett was stalking off, headed for a trail at the edge of the woods.

"I wonder if I should go after him," Carly said, biting her lower lip.

Mike Baldwin shook his head. "Let him blow off a little steam. If he's alone for a while, maybe he'll cool down."

Carly looked toward the trail for a moment, sighed, and said, "Maybe he does need to be by himself. Only Brett can work this out."

"What exactly happened with the brakes?" Frank asked, hoping to get Mike and Carly thinking about something besides Brett.

96

Mike knelt beside the bike. "Look at the front cable," he said. "It's been cut through partway. When Brett was pumping the brakes on the downhill, the tension on the cable must have made the wire snap the rest of the way."

Frank and Joe leaned in to see where Mike was pointing. The thin wire cable on the front brake was clearly cut on one side and frayed through on the other.

"Brett's lucky," Frank said with a low whistle. Under his breath, Frank said to Joe, "Are you thinking what I'm thinking?"

"Rich Alexander," Joe stated flatly.

Mike wanted to take the bike back to the pit. Carly agreed to go along with him, even though she gave Frank, Joe, and Chet a last reluctant look.

"Keep your eyes peeled for Brett, okay?" she asked. "He may come back and need to talk."

Frank nodded. "No problem." After they were gone, he shook his head and said, "Something doesn't seem right here. Why is it always Brett's bikes that are getting messed up and stolen?"

Another heat of the cross-country was barreling toward the finish line as Frank, Chet, and Joe stood in the clearing at the bottom of the trail.

"That's a good question," Joe said. "Why don't we sit down somewhere and hash this out." He led the way off the course toward some picnic tables set up next to the refreshment stands beside the finish line. The three friends each got a drink and sat down to discuss the latest series of events.

"We know that Rich Alexander has the motive, and the evidence points to him as the one committing the sabotage." Frank laid it out. "He was the last one to ride on the water ski before Moreno's accident, and I saw him switching the trail markers back after I almost flew off that cliff."

"Are you sure that was Rich?" Chet asked. "I mean, you know the guy was wearing Rich's goggles, but was it really him?"

Frank thought for a moment and tried to remember back to the accident. "The guy was wearing a helmet, so I didn't really get a good look at his face. But I saw dark hair, and I'm pretty sure I would recognize Alexander. He was wearing Apex shorts, and he was riding an Apex bike."

"There's only one problem. If you were going to do what Rich did," Joe countered, "and switch those markers, would you be so obvious?"

"He's right!" said Chet. He took a long sip of his soda. "Joe's got a good point."

Frank leaned back and crossed his arms. "So what's your theory?"

"Yeah, Chet," Joe chimed in. "Tell us the Morton Hypothesis."

"I don't exactly have a theory," Chet sputtered. "But Frank's right: Brett's the one whose bikes have been wrecked. No one else. Sure, Moreno went down in the waterskiing accident, and Frank almost went over the cliff. But it's only Brett's bikes that have been damaged."

"There's just one problem," Frank said, going over the case in his mind. "What about Moreno? Remember he lost his gears in the very first heat."

Chet looked downcast. "I guess you're right," he said glumly.

Frank stared off into the nearby woods. Somewhere in there, he knew Brett was doing some serious thinking. If Frank was right, the hotshot racer was trying to come to grips with the pressure he was under—both from his father and from the other competitors. Maybe he was even trying to decide if quitting really was the right thing.

"It's true," Frank said now, thinking aloud. "Except for Moreno's accident, Brett's been the victim all along."

"Which doesn't fit in at all with this rivalry between Moreno and Alexander," Chet pointed out.

"You don't really think he would sabotage his own bikes?" Joe asked. "Do you?"

Frank looked back and forth between Chet and Joe. "Think about it. What if you were Brett, and the pressure of being a pro at such a young age was getting to you? What if you knew you couldn't just quit because then your dad would be really mad at you? Maybe this was Brett's way of getting off the circuit without letting his father down."

Joe and Chet listened carefully, and when Frank was done, Joe shook his head. "I don't know, Frank. It seems a little far-fetched to me."

"There's only one way we can find out if Frank is right," Chet put in. "Ask Brett himself. See if he comes clean."

"Okay," Joe agreed. "Let's do it."

Frank nodded, got up from the picnic table, and tossed his empty drink cup into a nearby trash can. Then he began to walk toward the clearing at the base of the cross-country course.

Joe and Chet quickly caught up with Frank. The three friends found the path that Brett had taken into the woods. Soon, though, the trail reached a dead end, and they were deep in the forest. There was no trace of Brett.

"It's amazing how desolate these mountains get as soon as you leave the world behind," Joe said quietly.

Birds called out from high above. The wind whistled through the pine needles. Otherwise, the forest was deathly quiet.

"Brett!" Frank called out, breaking the silence. "Where are you? We want to talk to you."

There was no response. But Chet pointed off to

their right, where a flash of tan appeared in the otherwise green, gray, and brown woods.

"What's that?" Chet asked. "Brett!" he cried. "Where are you?"

To his left, Joe heard footsteps in the woods, the sound of twigs breaking on the forest floor. "Brett? Is that you?"

"Who is it?" came Brett's voice.

"Where are you?" Frank demanded.

Up ahead, Brett appeared. He stood some distance away, hidden by the pines. "Can't you guys see I don't want to talk to anyone?"

"We want to help," Chet offered. "We know what you did."

"What do you mean?" Brett demanded.

Frank saw the young racer take a few steps toward them. "We know about the sabotage," Frank said. "Why don't we go back and work this all out with your dad? I'm sure he'd understand if you want to quit."

"I don't know what you're talking about," Brett called out.

Joe put his hand on Frank's arm. "Look," he whispered.

At that moment, Frank heard a rustling sound in the trees to his right. He turned to see the same flash of tan Chet had noticed before.

"Tha-a-a-t's—" Chet sputtered, standing still in his tracks.

"Not a person," Joe confirmed.

Out of the woods crept a huge mountain lion. Frank caught his breath and motioned to Brett to stop. He had to keep the racer from stepping into the lion's path.

But the cat wasn't interested in Brett. It took a long look at Frank, Joe, and Chet and readied itself to leap—right at them.

11 Runaway Snowplow

"Don't move," Joe whispered.

Slowly, the mountain lion raised itself on its hind legs and pawed the air. In the silent woods, the lion's growl sounded like a deadly roar.

"I told you we should take those warnings about the wildlife seriously," said Chet in a low tone.

"Has anyone here done any lion taming?" Frank asked nervously. "I sure haven't."

Brett was about to take a step toward the Hardys when Joe motioned him to stop. "What are you doing?" he hissed.

"Trying to distract it," Brett offered.

Just then, the lion swished its tail and growled at Brett, baring its fangs.

"Don't bother," said Joe. "He's got an attention span a mile long. And it's focused on us!"

Joe knew that one swipe of the lion's paw could knock him flat. He didn't even want to think about the lion's claws and its fangs. Joe's heart began to pound triple time.

"One wrong move," he whispered to Frank and Chet, "and we're in deep trouble."

"I don't think we've got a lot of time to come up with a plan," said Frank.

As if it had understood Frank, the lion took two steps toward Frank, Chet, and Joe and then turned to Brett. Apparently it decided that Brett would make the tastiest meal, because the lion started walking toward him.

"He's stalking Brett!" Chet whispered hoarsely. "Quick, we've got to do something."

"Brett," Joe called out. "Whatever you do, don't move."

"Easier said than done," Brett said.

Joe searched the surrounding area for some kind of weapon. In a flash, his eyes lit upon a thick branch that had fallen into the underbrush to his right. He knelt down and reached for it, trying not to attract the lion's attention. His fingertips met the wood, and he held the branch aloft.

"I'm going to toss this stick," said Joe. "I won't hit the lion, but maybe I'll scare it off."

"Are you crazy?" Frank said. "The lion's going to jump right at Brett!"

"It's our only chance," said Joe. He threw the branch. The lion turned toward it and growled at Joe.

"Run!" Joe cried to Brett.

Brett raced to the right. Then, in a split second, Joe had another idea. He quickly grabbed another stick and threw it at the lion's rear. The lion raced into the woods, obviously scared off by the attack.

"All right!" Chet cried. "Let's get out of here."

Frank, Joe, and Chet sprinted out of the woods, with Brett at their heels. "Man, was that close," Frank said when they were safely back at the picnic tables where they'd had their soda just a while earlier.

"You're not kidding," said Joe. "You okay?" he asked Brett.

The young racer bent over to catch his breath. "Yeah," he said. "But that's enough near-death experiences for one day!"

Brett laughed, and Joe, Frank, and Chet all chimed in. Joe was happy to see the racer laughing and smiling again, but soon Brett's face returned to its usual serious expression.

"You want to talk about it?" Joe asked. "Maybe we can help."

Brett shook his head. "I don't think so. You guys are my pals, but you don't know the half of what I'm going through."

"Maybe we do," Chet said.

Collapsing onto a picnic bench, Brett rested his

105

head in his hands. Joe looked with sympathy at the young competitor. Around them, spectators were enjoying the last heats of the day, chatting among themselves about the winners and losers. But here, the leader of the Annihilator himself was crashing under the weight of all his pressure.

"Wouldn't it help to talk about it?" Joe asked him quietly.

"I've got a theory," Frank said, trying to sound lighthearted. "Joe says it's kind of crazy, but hey"—Frank shrugged—"maybe I'm wrong."

"What's your theory?" Brett asked.

"That you sabotaged your own bikes," Frank said, suddenly serious, "so you could get out of the competition without disappointing your dad."

Brett's blue eyes were wide. "That's beyond crazy," he sputtered. "It's downright stupid. What if I got caught? I'd ruin my whole future. I don't think so."

"Brett," said Joe. "Except for Moreno's derailleur back in that first downhill heat, you're the only one who's had trouble with his bikes. Sure, other stuff has happened around here, but that could just be to distract us from what counts."

"You're saying I did all that other stuff, too?" Brett demanded. "Wow. And I thought you guys were my friends."

Joe was about to give up when something important occurred to him. "You were alone with that bike, and you were the last person to use it. When Carly was done with her check, the brakes were fine. But by the time you rode it, the brake cable had been cut through."

Frank picked up on Joe's line of reasoning. "That fact alone makes you look pretty guilty."

Brett's eyes moved from Frank to Joe to Chet. Finally, he hung his head and mumbled, "I know you must think I'm a real creep or something."

"We don't," Joe insisted. "Why don't you tell us what happened?"

Slowly, Brett began his confession. "I did fix the bike. I rigged the suspension to fail, and I cut through the brake cable. Carly helped me. We did it just enough so that the brakes would go at the very end of the race, and I planned on taking that wipeout. My dad didn't even care that I'd been hurt! All he cared about was how I'd perform in the next race. I also set the fire that burned up my bike. I left the note so you guys would think someone was after you. Carly made up that story about my other bike being stolen."

Chet let out a low whistle. Joe saw how hard it was for Brett to admit to all this. The young racer's eyes grew cloudy with remorse.

"What's going to happen to me?" he wailed. "They won't put me in jail, will they?"

Frank tried to reassure Brett. "I really doubt it. But you're going to have to tell your father and Julia Alvarado."

"We cracked the case!" Chet announced proudly.

"Not so fast," said Joe. "Something doesn't feel right. Even if Brett sabotaged his bikes, that doesn't explain the switched trail marker, the loosened screw in Moreno's derailleur, or the waterskiing accident. What can you tell us about those incidents, Brett?" he said, turning to the racer.

"Not much, I'm afraid," Brett stated flatly. "What I did was stupid, sure, but I wouldn't have tried to hurt anybody. I'm telling you, I just wanted to be able to drop out of the races without looking like a quitter to my dad."

"That leaves us with none other than Rich Alexander," Frank said. "The question is, where is the guy? And what's he planning next?"

Later that night, the Hardys, Chet, Mike, Brett, and Carly sat around a picnic table by the lake. The competition's organizers had put together another barbecue, and afterward they were going to show video highlights of the day's races in the resort lounge. Brett had confessed everything to his father and Alvarado. As a result, he'd been eliminated from the competition as well as all races for the rest of the year. But next year he could come back and race again—if he wanted to.

At first, Mike had been upset and confused, but

finally he began to understand. Carly and Brett made him see what the extreme pressure had been doing to him. Now, all three were making plans for a vacation in the area as soon as the Annihilator was finished.

"And Disneyland, too," Brett said, his eyes twinkling. "We can't leave until we've seen Disneyland!"

Joe was happy to see his friend looking so relieved. He wished he and Frank could be as relaxed. They'd rerun their cross-country heat late that afternoon and hunted for Alexander afterward, but there still was no sign of their suspect. Justine Kaplan had no idea where he was either. His rental car was gone from the space in front of his cabin. And Con Riley had called to tell them that the bullet was from a starter gun, but the prints on them hadn't turned up any traceable suspects. All in all, Frank and Joe were at square one as far as solving the case was concerned. After tomorrow, the races would be over, and the suspect would go free. It was frustrating, but what could they do?

"We'll just have to wait for him to turn up," Joe said aloud.

"Alexander," Frank said, reading his brother's thoughts. He put down his piece of barbecued chicken and wiped his hands on a napkin. "I've got an idea," he said. "If Alexander won't come to us, why don't we go to him?"

"What do you mean?" Joe asked in a low voice.

"Since he's gone, wouldn't this be a good time to check out his cabin?"

"I like that idea," said Joe, grinning. "I like it a lot."

While Brett, Mike, and Carly talked among themselves, Frank and Joe quietly filled in Chet on their plan.

"I'll go back to our place and pick up the lock-pick tool," said Joe. "Meet you at Alexander's cabin."

Cutting through the woods back to his cabin, Joe was careful to listen for any sign that he was being followed—by Alexander or the local wildlife.

In the distance, Joe heard a loud rumbling sound, like a large engine idling. He figured it must be a sanitation truck coming to clear away rubbish. As he came out of the woods and into a clearing beside his cabin, Joe saw twin headlights and was blinded for a moment by their glare.

"What the—?" Joe said, holding up a hand to his eyes to shield himself from the light.

At first Joe thought that the garbage truck must have stopped by his cabin to empty the trash. But then, beyond the glare of the lights, Joe realized that it wasn't a garbage truck at all. It was a snowplow, and its big blade was lowered, prepared to shove everything out of its way—including Joe!

110

12 Caught—
Red-Handed!

If Joe Hardy didn't move fast, he was going to become next year's snowpack!

"Hey!" Joe cried. He tried waving his arms to catch the driver's attention. "Watch where you're going," he called out.

The man driving the plow kept coming. By now, Joe was frantic. There was no more than ten feet between him and the plow. He searched for an escape. On either side of him were the cabins. The plow was coming right up between them, leaving him no room. Joe had two choices: run into the woods and hope the guy didn't chase him or jump up onto the shovel and escape over the top of the plow.

Joe decided to jump. With an earsplitting cry,

he leapt up onto the metal shovel, grasping in the dark for a handhold.

For a second, he clung to the top of the blade, then found the strength to pull himself up. Swinging his legs onto the top of the plow, Joe discovered a foothold on the other side where the shovel was attached to the truck.

Joe stood on the metal block between the blade and the truck, wobbling, trying to get his balance. Then he turned to get a look at the driver. Through the windshield, he saw the guy was wearing a ski mask. As soon as the driver saw Joe, he jumped from the cab of the truck, leaving it running.

"Hey!" Joe cried out. He scrambled to get down from the snowplow without falling beneath its tires. The driver was running toward the road that ran in front of the cabins.

Now or never, Joe thought. Taking a deep breath, he jumped from the plow, trying to leap as far out as possible.

With a thud, he landed a safe distance from the plow. He raced to the road and spotted the man who'd been driving the plow. The man was running down the road, and Joe could clearly see that the man ran with a limp.

"Stop him!" Joe cried out, but there was no one on the road to hear him. Before Joe could do anything, the man pulled a bike from the bushes, hopped on, and rode off into the darkness. Joe stopped running and stood there, his heart pounding, feeling completely helpless.

Meanwhile, the snowplow had stalled out. Joe raced back to it, hopped on board, and took the truck out of gear. After a quick inspection, he realized that the machinery did not require a key to turn it on.

"So that's how he managed to steal this thing," Joe said aloud. "It was as easy as pushing this little button."

Joe quickly figured out how to back up the plow. Once he was out on the road, he cut the engine and left it parked beside the cabin. Then he raced inside, got his lock-pick tool, and hurried over to Alexander's cabin where Chet and Frank were waiting for him.

"Wait'll you hear what happened," Joe whispered to his two friends. Joe filled them both in about the deadly snowplow.

"You were lucky," Chet said. "Sure you're not hurt?"

"Positive," said Joe. He took a deep breath, reliving the moment when the snowplow came out of the darkness, barreling toward him. "Somehow the guy didn't nail me. Unfortunately, I didn't nail him either."

"You mean he got away?" Frank said. "How'd he manage that?"

"He took off on a bike," Joe said. "I never had a chance. But I'm sure it was Alexander."

"Why?" Frank asked.

"He had a limp. Remember that Alexander was injured when he went off course the other day," Joe reminded them.

Chet nodded. "Sure." He paused for a moment, then said, "But Moreno's got a limp, too, remember?"

Joe shot his friend an irritated look. "Moreno's not a suspect, remember?"

Chet shrugged. "Just trying to help."

Frank turned to them both. "If you two are done bickering, I'd like to go ahead with our plan. Chet, you wait out here and guard the place. Any sign of Alexander, just whistle three times. Like this."

Frank pursed his lips and gave one short whistle and two long. Chet practiced, imitating Frank. "Got it," Chet said.

"Okay," said Joe. "Let's do it."

Joe heaved himself up onto the porch that wrapped around the cabin. Heading for the back, Joe stopped at an open window.

"Check this out," he said to Frank. "We don't even need to break in."

Frank used his penknife to pop out the screen, and he and Joe quickly passed through. After they were inside, Joe flicked on the flashlight he'd brought and shone it around the room.

They were in the breakfast area. To the right was the kitchen and in front of them the living

114

room. There were books and magazines spread out on every available surface.

"You check here," Joe said. "I'll cover the bedroom."

Leaving Frank to sort through Alexander's mess, Joe headed for the bedroom. There, the stacks of magazines, books, records, and CDs were even messier than the living room. Joe wondered if the guy brought everything he owned with him!

Joe was careful not to disturb Alexander's mess. "Not that he'd notice," he said under his breath. He quickly searched the piles on the windowsill, then moved to the dresser and desk. There was nothing obvious, nothing linking Rich to the sabotage.

Moving from the piles to the dresser and desk drawers, Joe pulled out one after another and found nothing more than some T-shirts and underwear and resort stationery.

"Zero," came Frank's voice. He was standing in the doorway, a downcast expression on his face.

"Me, too," Joe said. He panned the room with his flashlight, searching for some kind of hiding place. "There's not even a closet in here," he said in frustration.

"It's in the hall," said Frank. "I already looked." He paused, then ran his hands through his hair. "We can't stay here all night. Rich is sure

115

to come back at some point. The cross-country is tomorrow, and he'll need his sleep."

"If we don't crack this case by tomorrow," Joe put in, "the Annihilator's going to be over, and our saboteur will get away scot-free."

"Well, there's nothing here," said Frank. "Come on." He stepped out of the doorway and started back down the hall that led to the living room.

Joe was about to follow his brother. But on a hunch, he darted into the bathroom. "I'm not giving up this easily," he said to Frank. "We still haven't searched here."

While Frank waited just outside the bathroom, Joe ran his flashlight around the small tiled room. He searched the medicine chest. Nothing. Then the storage under the sink. Again nothing. Finally, Joe lifted the cover off the back of the toilet tank. There, his flashlight picked up a plastic bag floating in the tank.

"Frank," called Joe. "Check this out!"

Inside his lock-pick kit was a pair of tweezers, which Joe used to remove the plastic bag. He held it out to Frank.

"The starter gun," Frank said, his voice a whisper.

"And a pocketknife," Joe pointed out. "Not to mention a spare round of ammo for the gun."

Frank let out a low whistle. "That's a lot of evidence."

Just then, Joe heard Chet's warning whistle.

116

Both Frank and Joe raced into the living room and peered out through the blinds. A car had driven up, and someone was getting out.

"Bad news," Joe whispered.

It was Rich Alexander. Joe and Frank were about to be caught in his cabin—red-handed.

13 A False Trail

"Get down," Frank Hardy hissed.

But it was too late. Alexander had turned on the lights. Frank and Joe were completely exposed.

"What on earth?" Rich stared at them both, his car keys jangling in his hand. "I think you guys got the wrong cabin."

"Very funny," said Joe. "Actually, I think we've got the right cabin. And the right guy."

"I don't know what you're talking about," Alexander said. He took a menacing step toward Joe. "But I'm not sure I even want to find out. Clear out," he bellowed. "Now!"

"Take it easy," Frank said, stepping between Joe and Rich.

Just then, Chet rushed through the front door,

his fists raised. "You guys okay? I heard someone yelling."

"That was me," said Alexander. "I was telling your friends to beat it. You can include yourself in that, too." Rich stood by the door and gave them all an angry look. "Well?"

"We're not leaving until we get some answers," Joe said hotly.

"You've got a lot of nerve," said Rich. "You want answers from me? You're the ones who broke into my cabin. You don't see me asking you for answers!"

"That's because we're not the ones who have been sabotaging the Annihilator!" said Joe.

"You little—" Rich lunged for Joe.

"Cut it out!" Frank cried. He put himself between Joe and Rich. "Now." With one hand on Joe's chest and the other on Alexander's arm, Frank was able to put some distance between them. "If you don't want to talk to us, then we'll call Julia Alvarado and she'll call the police, and you'll have to answer their questions. So what'll it be?"

Alexander made a face, obviously weighing his options. Finally, he took a step back from Frank and sat down on the sofa. With his hands resting on his knees and his eyes narrowed, he said, "Go ahead. I don't have anything to hide."

"What about this?" Joe asked. He held out the bag containing the starter gun, the knife, and the spare ammo. "It sure wasn't in plain sight."

"I have no idea what you're talking about," said Rich. "You want to explain yourselves?"

"What's in the bag?" Chet asked, his eyes focused on the object in Joe's hand.

Joe placed the bag on the table in front of Alexander and pointed to its contents. "Our theory is that an accomplice of yours used the starter gun to disrupt your hotdog heat with Trace Heller."

"And that you used that penknife to cut through the towrope on the water ski," Frank stated flatly.

"How convenient." Alexander smirked, and his eyes moved from Frank to Joe to Chet. "So you guys really are detectives, huh? Well, smart boys, did it occur to you that if I did all those things, I sure wouldn't leave the evidence around where someone could find it."

"Maybe you were going to get rid of it later," Chet put in.

"Or maybe someone's trying to frame me," said Alexander.

Joe pressed his lips together. "Like who?"

"Like Mauro Moreno," said Alexander. "He'd do anything to get back at me. That guy's been looking for revenge for three years—ever since Apex dropped him and signed me up. He even tried to get to Justine. She told me he asked her to lunch and started trying to make a deal with her. Said he'd be willing to leave Don Jackson if the pot was sweet enough."

"Is that why you were spying on Jackson?" Frank asked. "To make sure you stay on Kaplan's good side?"

Rich gave Frank a confused look. "I don't know what you're talking about. Spy on Jackson? Me?" He placed a palm to his chest and gave all three a questioning look. "That really takes the cake."

"We caught you coming out of their trailer," Joe reminded him. "You never did say what you were doing there."

"Sure I did," said Alexander. "I was checking out the Y-factor frames. So what? In three months, everyone's going to know what they look like. I just wanted to be the first. That's not spying."

Frank realized the racer had a point. He leaned over the coffee table and grabbed the plastic bag. "If you don't mind, we'd like to keep this stuff. Run some tests on it, you know."

Alexander shrugged his shoulders and scratched the back of his neck. "Be my guest." He stretched his arms above his head and yawned. "If that's all the questions you kids have, I'd like to hit the hay now. Big race tomorrow, you know, and it's been a long day already."

"Where were you all day anyway?" Joe asked. "We looked for you everywhere."

"Really?" Alexander smiled. "It must have bothered you that you couldn't find me. Well, to tell you the truth, I took a long bike ride to prepare for tomorrow and then I drove into town

121

to have dinner and catch a movie. Being around all these racers drives me crazy. I like to get out on my own, if you know what I mean."

"Yeah," said Joe. "Right."

"Come on," Frank urged. "We should let Rich get his rest."

Once they were outside, Chet and Joe turned to Frank. Both were obviously angry. "I can't believe we just walked right out of there," said Joe. "I had a million questions I could have asked. I'm sure we could have gotten the guy to break down."

"Joe's right," Chet said. "You didn't even ask him about the trail markers or the towrope."

Frank sighed. "I know. But chances are he would have just denied having done those things anyway." He shook his head. "Nope. If we're going to catch Rich Alexander, it'll have to be in the act."

"And tomorrow's our last chance to do just that," said Joe. "Let's hope we don't blow it."

The next day, the largest crowd in the history of the Annihilator had turned out to see the cross-country blowout. The start and finish lines were packed with spectators, and all the major newspapers and news stations in the area had sent reporters.

"I can't believe this crowd," said Joe. "I guess mountain biking is really catching on."

But Frank's mind wasn't on the banners, the

cameras, or the shouting fans. Instead, he kept his eyes peeled for any sign of trouble. He and Joe were both going to race that day. Frank was equally worried about catching the Wolf Mountain saboteur as he was about whether he could make it on the grueling twenty-mile race.

"There's Brett," Chet cried. "Hey, Brett!"

Brett was standing near the judges' table that was set up by the finish line. Beside the table, a booth had been set up for the media. Frank saw Mauro Moreno giving an interview. Behind him stood Rich Alexander along with Justine Kaplan. Trace Heller was hovering nearby. Obviously, all the key racers were doing their best to get media play.

"Come on," said Joe. "Let's say hello to Brett before we have to get ready to race."

None of the newspapers or stations seemed to be interested in talking to Brett, because he and Carly and Mike Baldwin were standing off to the side, all alone. Brett gave Joe, Frank, and Chet a big grin as they came over.

"Good luck, guys," he said. "We'll be here to cheer you on as you finish."

"Thanks," said Joe. "And thanks for fixing my bike, too. It's riding better than the day I bought it."

Mike beamed. "I've still got my touch. Who knows, maybe you'll even be a winner!"

"I doubt it," said Joe. "But I wouldn't miss it for the world. And I wouldn't miss this either," he added, his eyes sweeping the scene around him.

All around, reporters, camerapeople, and photographers were eating up the action. Frank watched as Rich Alexander gave an interview and then passed on the questions to Justine Kaplan, who was obviously a pro at dealing with the press. Since Moreno had finished his interview, he and Heller were leaving the press booth, not before Alexander gave them both a dirty look. Frank waited for something to happen between the three racers, but Heller pulled his friend's arm and led him away.

As Trace and Mauro were passing by, Mauro stopped. "Tough break, kid," he said to Brett. "Maybe next year, huh?" He dropped the duffel bag he was carrying and reached out to shake Brett's hand. At that moment, Frank happened to look down and what he saw shocked him.

Lying on top of Moreno's gear was a pair of neon blue and green goggles—just like the kind Rich Alexander wore. A sick feeling came over Frank as he watched Moreno joke with Brett.

What if it were Moreno who messed up the marker on the cross-country trail? Frank thought. Could Rich Alexander be right? Was Mauro Moreno really the Wolf Mountain saboteur?

14 Rock Slide

Pieces started clicking into place for Frank. Moreno had a limp and so did the man who drove the snowplow at Joe. Moreno could have cut his own towrope when it was his turn to water-ski. He could easily have stolen Rich's goggles or bought a pair of his own and worn them when he switched the markers, just to make the Hardys suspect Rich. Since Moreno had raced with Apex, it was likely that he still had Apex gear, such as the shorts and shirt Frank had spotted on the guy who switched the marker. And Moreno could even have worn a dark, curly wig to make Frank think he was Rich Alexander.

Those were a lot of *ifs*, but Frank was fairly bursting with the theories. He knew he had to talk to Joe, preferably before their race started.

Now they had to keep their eyes not only on Alexander but also on Moreno—just in case his theory was accurate.

While Joe chatted with Brett, Heller, and Moreno, Frank grabbed his brother's arm and pulled him away. He motioned for Chet to come over, too, after excusing himself from Mr. Baldwin.

"What's wrong?" Joe asked. "You getting cold feet or something? Your face is totally white."

"I've got to talk to you," Frank said. In low tones, he outlined his suspicions. All the while, Frank kept his eyes on Mauro Moreno, trying to decide if the racer was capable of taking his revenge against Alexander to such lengths.

"Something was never right about that guy," Chet confirmed. "He seemed too cocky for one."

Joe nodded in agreement. "True, but there's a difference between arrogance and what Frank's saying Moreno did. I still say Rich is our man."

"We can't stand here debating the issue," said Frank. "Moreno might hear us. Besides, the race is about to start."

"What'll we do?" Joe asked his brother. "This is the last race of the Annihilator. The Wolf Mountain saboteur is sure to strike. We've narrowed it down to Alexander or Moreno."

"We'll have to watch both of them," Frank said, putting on his helmet. "One of them is going to go after the other, that's for sure. I just hope we can keep up with them during the race.

Otherwise, it might happen while we're back in the pack."

"Not to worry," said Joe with determination. "I've been in training, remember?" He smiled and cracked his knuckles.

"Yeah, right," said Frank. Moreno was saying goodbye to Brett Baldwin now. Before he walked away, Mauro greeted Frank and Joe, while Trace Heller called out to the surrounding press, "Meet the next national champion, Mauro Moreno! Get your interviews before he's famous!"

Moreno punched his friend lightly on the arm. "Cut it out, Heller. Good luck, you guys," he said to Frank and Joe. "See you in the winner's circle. I plan to be there!" With that, Moreno and Heller strode off, chatting and laughing.

"Sure you do," said Frank under his breath. "We'll be there, too, watching your every move."

"I still say it's Alexander," said Joe, a little too loud. Moreno stopped dead in his tracks and turned around to look at the Hardys and Chet.

"Alexander who, what?" Mauro asked. "I heard a rumor going around that you kids aren't journalists at all, that you're detectives. If you suspect that Alexander is behind all the trouble here, you'd be dead right."

Frank tried to cover for them. He laughed. "Detectives? No way. We do think it's Alexander who's going to *win*. Our magazine is calling him the favorite. Can you give us a quote on that?"

"Are you kidding." Moreno shot Heller a huge

127

grin and said to Frank, "Rich Alexander couldn't win a soapbox derby racing against turtles. I'm going to beat him and prove to everyone what an old man he really is."

"All *right!*" Heller cried. He and Moreno exchanged a high five. "Dude!"

Both racers burst out laughing, then went on their way. Once they were out of earshot, Frank turned to glare at Joe. "Nice work," he said. "You may have just blown our cover for good."

"He didn't know what I was talking about," Joe grumbled. "Besides, you covered really well."

An announcement came over the PA system. "All racers please come to the starting line. The final cross-country race begins in five minutes. Repeat: All racers to the starting line to take your positions."

"This is it," said Joe. "Ready?"

Frank nodded. "I think so."

"Good luck, you guys," said Chet. "I'll be waiting for you at the finish line."

Joe hopped on his bike and started cruising toward the starting position. Frank followed his brother, moving slowly through the crowd. In his head, Frank tried to remember the course. The night before, Joe had shown it to Frank on one of the Annihilator maps. He knew that it started out along the same route as the mini-cross-country he'd raced the day before. But past the point where he'd taken the wrong turn, the longer course went farther down into the canyon instead of climbing back up the mountain the way the shorter cross-country trail did. Then, the trail followed a mountain stream for a short distance before it came to a series of switchbacks that went up another mountain. From that mountain, a steep grade led back down the other side, then up a grueling last incline to another ridge that led back to the resort. It was the last climb that had Frank worried. After racing for fifteen miles, would he be able to make a five-mile ascent back into the mountains? he wondered.

But he had no time to worry. He and Joe were taking their places along with nearly fifty other racers at the starting line.

"Just try to stick to my pace," said Joe, putting on his goggles. "I'll keep us within shouting distance of Moreno and Alexander. If anything goes wrong, we'll be close enough to catch one of them."

Frank nodded, swallowed, and wrapped his fingers around the handlebars, checking the brakes on his bike one last time. To his left, at the far end of the pack, Moreno was giving Heller the thumbs up. To Frank's right, Rich Alexander had a serious, intense look on his face. The pack was quiet as the race official prepared to count down the start. Finally, he raised his gun and counted the last five seconds.

"Four, three, two, one!"

The starting gun cracked the air.

"We're off!" Joe Hardy shouted.

From the start, Moreno, Heller, and Alexander took the lead. Frank struggled to keep up with Joe, who was at the back of the first pack.

"You can do it!" Joe shouted to his brother. "Pump it!"

His legs were burning with the effort, but Frank pushed on. The racers cruised down into the woods, where the cool breeze played across Frank's cheeks. Frank had no time to enjoy the moment though. Joe's legs were pumping, and Frank did his best to keep his movements up to speed with Joe's. He knew that if he could just match his brother's pace, he'd be able to stay with the pack.

The first steep grade down almost did Frank in. Before he knew it, the pack behind him had surrounded him. What was he doing wrong?

"Shift up," Joe urged, shouting to Frank.

Switching to a higher gear, Frank was able to get the proper leverage. A burst of speed sent him flying forward, out of the pack, and toward Joe. Frank quickly realized that going downhill he'd have to pedal just as hard as on the uphills or else he'd lose momentum.

"I should have been out training with Joe," Frank said through gritted teeth.

Finally, at the bottom of the grade, Frank was able to pull abreast of his brother. Not more than fifty feet ahead, Frank saw Moreno still in the lead, with Heller, Alexander, and another two riders just behind.

"Pretty close, huh?" Joe asked, panting. His face was bright red, and the sweat was dripping off his nose. "Get ready for a tough climb, but then it's nice and flat for five or six miles."

Frank grunted. Half a mile later, they came to the place where someone had shifted the marker in the mini-cross-country. Instead of going left, the course veered right and took a steep uphill. Frank couldn't even see the top.

"How long a climb uphill is it?" he groaned.

"Downshift," Joe panted. "You don't want to know."

The muscles on Frank's legs burned, and he felt as if he'd never catch his breath. "I won't make it," he said once they were halfway up the hill.

"You don't have a choice," said Joe.

In a last burst of energy, Frank was able to see the top. The sound of running water to the right made his throat ache with thirst, but he knew he couldn't stop for a drink. Not now. Finally, when they had reached the top and the trail leveled off, Frank grabbed for the water bottle attached to his frame and took a long sip.

Joe was doing the same. "Having fun yet?" he asked his brother.

"Sure. But the next time I'm expected to do championship racing, tell me a few months ahead, okay? Might be good to train for it."

The flat miles of the course gave Frank and Joe the chance to make up for the time they had lost on the uphill. The Hardys quickly came out of the pack and found a pocket between the leaders and the group behind them. Moreno, Alexander, and Heller traded the lead as they raced along the fast-running mountain stream.

"Still no sign of trouble," Frank panted, "which is a relief, since I'm not sure I could catch anyone in the condition I'm in."

"No pain, no gain," Joe joked.

Soon, they were coming to the series of switchbacks that climbed the mountain. "How tall is this thing anyway?" Frank wanted to know.

"Six thousand feet," said Joe. "But we're already at three, so it's only another three you have to climb."

"Oh, is that all?" Frank groaned.

Moreno and Heller disappeared from view, and Frank concentrated on keeping his legs moving. Once or twice, Frank noticed Alexander on the trail above, ahead of them, but just barely. The canyon got steeper and steeper as they climbed, and soon they were creeping along, with cliffs on their left and a breathtaking drop on their right.

"Nice view," said Joe.

"If you don't look down," Frank said dryly.

The racers spread out behind them. Ahead, Frank couldn't spot Heller or Moreno anymore. Since the switchbacks were at least fifty feet above, it was hard to tell which racers were in the lead or even where they were. Alexander remained twenty feet or so ahead of them.

Frank was concentrating on the trail and catching up to the leaders when suddenly rocks started to fall from above, crashing down onto the trail in front of them.

"What the—" Frank looked up and saw that even bigger boulders were rolling down the mountain.

"What's going on?" Joe cried out, steering his bike to avoid the falling rocks.

In horror, Frank saw rocks and dust careening down the mountain, right toward them. "We're about to get pummeled," Frank shouted, "by a rock slide!"

15 Crossing the Rapids

"Watch out!" Joe Hardy cried, holding his hand above his head. "This whole mountainside could go!"

Rocks and other debris were still falling from above. A huge boulder bounced off the mountainside, and Frank and Joe were able to narrowly avoid being hit by it. Joe could see that fifty feet ahead of them the trail was clear. But right in front of them, the rock slide had sidelined Alexander, who was lying sideways below his bike, an awful grimace on his face.

"Come on!" Joe shouted. "We've got to help him."

Frank and Joe plowed through the landslide. They hopped off their bikes and ran to the injured racer. Frank shoved Alexander's bike

134

aside, and then he and Joe each grabbed one of Alexander's arms.

"Hurry!" Joe urged.

The three stumbled through the rainfall of debris just in time to see a huge chunk of the mountainside collapse onto the trail. The racers lagging behind them would be trapped on the other side unless they could ride over the barrier.

"How did that happen?" Frank Hardy wanted to know when they got to the other side.

Joe's heart was pounding. "I don't want to know," he said, looking back. Just as he was about to return his gaze to the trail in front of them, he made out a figure on the switchback above them. The racer had stopped and was about to get back on his bike.

"Look," Joe said to Frank, craning his neck. "Isn't that Moreno?"

"You bet it is. Is something wrong with his bike, do you think?" Frank asked.

"I doubt it," said Joe. "I'm afraid I think he's the guy who caused that landslide just now!"

Moreno's movements were hurried and furtive and he never bothered looking back.

"He must have been going after Alexander," Joe said. "And trying to slow down the rest of us."

"We're going to nail that creep!" Frank said firmly. "Come on!"

The Hardys both grabbed their bikes. Alexander tried to get onto his, but the pain was obviously too much for him to bear. "Go after him," he said, leaning against his bike. "I'm going to have to catch up with you guys."

Joe nodded and got back on his bike. "We won't let him get away with it," he promised Rich with a pat on the racer's shoulder. With that, he and Frank took the trail. Ahead, Moreno, who had lost his lead to Heller, was rapidly trying to make up the time.

"Do you think Moreno knows we saw him?" Joe asked, panting wildly.

"Could be," said Frank, the pain showing on his face. "With Heller so far ahead, that would make us the only witnesses—besides Alexander."

"If we catch up with him, I'll bet anything he goes after us just like he did Alexander," Joe said.

"Without a doubt," Frank agreed. "The guy just doesn't want to try winning fair and square."

Gasping for air, his muscles burning, Joe hunkered down over his handlebars, his eyes on Moreno, who was still more than two hundred yards ahead. Finally, the steep grade evened out at the mountaintop. The trail became a series of twists and turns as it followed the ridge that would take them, eventually, back to the resort.

Up ahead, Frank saw that Moreno had passed Heller. The uphill ride seemed to have taken its toll on Heller, and his pace had slowed a bit. Joe gritted his teeth and forced his screaming muscles to close the gap between them.

By now, Joe was almost abreast of Heller. As he was about to pass the racer, Trace the Mace looked over his shoulder, saw Joe, and decided to make a defensive move. He veered to the left, straight into Joe's path.

"Eyaah!" Joe cried, losing control for a second. "Watch what you're doing," he growled.

Heller simply leered at Joe. "This race isn't for amateurs," he shot back. "If you can't stand the heat, stay off the trail!"

Joe had regained his balance, but Heller took the opportunity to push ahead, his long hair flying in the wind. Frank was just behind Joe, and all three of them trailed Moreno.

There was no end in sight to the twists and turns of the trail. They were above the treeline by now, and all around was an incredible view of the mountains nearby. After about two miles of level racing, Joe had caught his breath from the uphill climb and was ready to put on some speed to try catching up with Moreno.

"Check out my moves," Joe cried out to Frank, pedaling fast and switching into high gear.

With an earsplitting war cry, Joe pounded the trail. He inched close to Heller and—giving the racer a wide berth—passed him.

"All right!" came Frank's cry.

Moreno was now within sight, no more than fifty yards ahead. Frank pedaled furiously and pulled up beside Joe, giving his brother a tight grin.

"We left Heller in the dirt," Frank panted.

"Let's see if we really have what it takes," Joe grunted. Switching gears again, Joe ignored the burn that raced up his legs, and he pushed on. *Closer, closer.* Finally, he was actually in Moreno's draft. Joe caught the wind and found he could ease up a bit on his pedaling. He'd read about the move but had never actually done it before.

Moreno turned around to see Joe and Frank hot on his trail. He looked downright surprised. Then he sneered. "You stupid kids," Mauro said, "So you want to try playing with the big boys!"

The racer veered to the left and slowed enough so that all of them were abreast. Heller rode up on the right, and Joe had an awful realization: He and Frank were about to become a human sandwich, squeezed together by Moreno and Heller.

"Watch it!" Joe cried to Frank. The two brothers dropped back just in time. Moreno veered toward Heller, clipping Heller's rear tire. The racer went down, head over heels, in a terrible spinout.

Joe looked back, ready to slow down and help him, when Frank called out, "Don't worry about him. We've got to nail our guy."

Moreno was cruising along at an easy pace, confident of his lead, when Joe blazed up to him. "Nice try, dude," he cried out. "But you're going to have to take us out if you want to get away with your little tricks!"

Giving Joe a dirty look, Moreno tightened his jaw and pushed ahead.

"Cool!" said Frank, barreling along to meet up with Joe. "That leaves Moreno and us. Two against one doesn't seem right, but he hasn't exactly been playing fair either."

"So true," said Joe.

For another mile or so, the Hardys kept up. Twice, Joe looked behind to see Heller and Alexander, far back on the trail, trying desperately to stay in the race.

"We've just got to stay on Moreno's back," Joe said, pumping hard. But gradually Moreno's conditioning paid off and he widened the gap between them.

Half a mile later, the trailhead split in two and Moreno was suddenly nowhere in sight. The Annihilator sign clearly marked that they should go left, but Joe noticed fresh tire tracks off to the right.

"Check this out," Joe said to his brother as he slowed down.

"What's he doing?" asked Frank.

"If I read the map right, this trail meets up with the other one closer to the finish. If a rider has the guts to try it, it could be a shortcut."

"That guy will do anything to win!" Frank exclaimed.

"He must have figured we would be too far back to notice which trail he took," Joe said grimly.

"We don't have any choice," Frank urged. "We have to follow him."

"Be careful!" Joe cautioned. "We're in for a rough ride."

The trail narrowed into a hiking path, and there was just enough clearance between the pines once they got below the treeline. On their right, Joe heard the sound of rushing water and figured it must be the upper portion of the mountain river they'd biked along earlier in the race.

"How's it going?" Joe called out to his brother. "You still there?"

"You bet I am," said Frank. "Won't Moreno be surprised when we catch up with him!"

"He won't like it, that's for sure," Joe agreed. "He must be really desperate to win if he's willing to cause a landslide and risk getting caught cheating by going off trail."

"Just imagine, then, how far he'll go when he discovers we're on to him," Frank said, catching his breath. "Out here with no witnesses," he added darkly.

Joe realized Frank had a point. It wasn't a pleasant thought. "We'll just have to keep our eyes out for his dirty tricks and for any traps."

By now, the sound of running water was getting louder. Far below them at the foot of the mountain, Joe spotted the thin trickle of a river.

"What's he got in mind?" Joe wondered aloud.

The trail they were on dead-ended in a clearing. Below them, the stream rushed by on its way to the waterfall, which Joe could see off to their right. A huge tree trunk had fallen across the river, and Moreno was already cruising over it. When he got to the other side he stopped and pulled out what looked to be a crudely drawn map. He nodded a few times, then quietly folded up the map and rode off again.

"Did you see that?" asked Joe.

"He must've scoped out this shortcut when none of his attempts to get rid of Alexander worked," Frank said.

The brothers looked at the slippery trunk and the rushing water below.

"What are we going to do?" Frank practically shouted. "We can't just let him get away. And we're too far off trail to go back now."

"Besides," Joe added. "If Alexander has managed to catch up by the time Moreno rejoins the trail, there's no telling what he'll do."

The two boys stood for a moment, thinking.

"I'm going over," said Joe. "You follow. If you get into trouble, give a yell."

The trunk lay between two banks of the river, which was at least twenty feet below. Joe decided to walk his bike, since he wasn't sure he had the balance to ride over it. He hoisted the bike onto his shoulder and tested the trunk. "It's pretty strong," he said to Frank.

"Hurry," Frank urged. "Moreno's getting away."

Joe took a few hesitant steps, searching for his balance. The trunk was wet, and he tried not to think about the river rushing by below. With a deep breath, he continued across. Soon he was halfway across and feeling more confident. By the time he got to the other side, Joe wasn't even thinking about the river anymore or the waterfall. His eyes were searching the woods ahead for a sign of Moreno and the trail he must have taken out of there.

"Joe!" Frank called out. "Help!"

Joe turned just in time to see Frank—halfway across the trunk, desperately trying to hold on to his bike with one hand and keep his balance with the other.

"I'm going to fall!" Frank cried.

The bike slipped from Frank's hand and crashed into the river below. Joe watched in horror as the bike spun down the river, headed for the falls. When he turned back to look at Frank, Joe's stomach flopped yet again.

Frank was swaying on the trunk, back and forth, trying to keep his balance. Before Joe could do anything to help him, his brother started to fall—right into the rushing water below!

16 Winner at Wolf Mountain

At the last second, Frank grabbed onto the tree trunk and stopped his fall. Below him, he could see his feet dangling in midair. The sound of the waterfall was a deadly reminder of what would happen to him if he let go of the trunk.

Clutching madly, Frank searched for some sort of grip. The trunk's bark was wet and slippery, but Frank found a knothole and dug his fingers into it. Now he was hanging on mostly by his right hand. With his left hand, he reached around to the other side of the trunk, hoping to hoist himself back onto the tree.

"I'm coming!" Joe cried. "Don't move."

Frank felt the trunk give slightly as Joe stepped onto it from his end. His handhold slipped for a moment, and he was sure he was a goner, but in the last second, Frank regained his grip.

He was still struggling to get his left hand around the top of the trunk when he felt Joe reach for it.

"On three," Joe said. "One, two—"

Frank used his right hand for leverage and pulled with all his might.

"Three!"

The move worked. Joe managed to keep his balance on the trunk and still pull on Frank's arm hard enough that the older Hardy was able to hoist first his left leg up around the trunk and then the rest of his body.

"That was close," Joe said, wiping the sweat from his forehead.

"Too close," said Frank, trying not to look down. Below, there wasn't a sign of his bike— just white water and, off in the distance, the falls. Even though he was still weak in the knees, Frank crouched on the trunk. "Let's get out of here," he said. "We've lost a lot of time. Besides, I can't wait to see Moreno's face when he sees he hasn't lost us."

Joe was about to scuttle backward on the trunk when he said, "There's just one problem."

Frank scanned Joe's face. "What's that?"

"We only have one bike."

Frank bit his lower lip and thought for a moment. "So? We'll both ride on yours," he said finally. "We used to do that when we were kids."

"Frank, you weigh a hundred and fifty-five pounds," Joe pointed out.

"Are you trying to tell me something?" Frank asked with a grin.

Joe had to laugh. "Right. I brought you all the way out here to the middle of nowhere, practically over a waterfall, to let you know you should go on a diet!"

Both Frank and Joe were smiling now. "Come on," said Frank. "Time's a'wasting!"

Joe squirmed backward off the trunk while Frank crawled along behind him. Soon, they'd rescued Joe's bike from where he'd left it. Frank climbed on the handlebars, and Joe craned his neck to see around his brother. It was slow going but faster than it would be if Frank ran alongside the bike.

"Where'd he get to?" Joe wondered aloud.

The trail on this side of the river took them into a more barren ridgeline. Eventually, the trees gave way to small pines and soon disappeared altogether, leaving only sagebrush and, in a few places, cactus plants.

"We should be able to spot him easily up here," said Frank.

They were now riding along a plateau.

"There he is!" Frank cried. "Just up ahead."

"Look at him," Joe said with disgust. "He's cruising along like he's out for a Sunday ride in the country."

Frank snorted in agreement. "He thinks he's

got everyone fooled. He's not bothering to put any speed into it."

Just then, Moreno must have sensed their approach, because he suddenly tensed and whipped his head around. Disbelief, then anger crossed his face. His head snapped forward again and, crouching lower on his bike, he surged ahead.

"Get him!" Frank shouted.

"I'm trying!" Joe answered, breathing hard. Frank's added weight was sapping his energy.

"It's no good," Joe panted finally. "I can't get up the speed."

Frank knew what he had to do. "I'm going right, you veer left," he instructed. With a yelp, he flung himself forward and as far to the right as he could. He hit the dirt with a jarring thud, rolling over and over until he came to a stop. He took a moment to take a deep breath to clear his head, then carefully pushed himself up into a kneeling position. He raised his head to see Joe's progress.

What he saw caused fear to tighten in his stomach. Joe had managed to catch up with Moreno all right. They were riding side by side. But Mauro's plan was terrifyingly clear to Frank. Moreno was trying to force Joe off the trail. And up here, Frank knew, that meant forcing Joe off the side of the mountain!

Frank jumped to his feet and raced after the

riders. He quickly realized there was no way for him to catch up on foot.

"Watch out, Joe!" Frank shouted helplessly.

Moreno tapped Joe once again. This time, Joe couldn't recover and the back wheels of his bike lost their grip. Joe instantly lurched off the left side of his bike as the machine flew right, down into the gaping chasm. For a moment, Frank thought Joe's move did the trick. But the momentum must have been too much. Frank gasped in horror as he watched his brother slide off the edge of the cliff!

"Joe! Joe!" he shouted, racing toward the sheer drop. He peered over the side where he had seen his brother fall, and his mouth fell open in shock.

"Shhhhh," Joe whispered, a finger to his lips. He was crouched on a ledge below. The younger Hardy had managed to slide a few dozen feet, clutching at weeds, rocks, and dirt to slow his progress. He was completely covered in dirt. His bike was nowhere to be seen. It had taken the long drop down.

Relief flooded through Frank. He looked quizzically at his brother, then quickly guessed Joe's plan. Frank glanced ahead to see Moreno getting off his bike. Frank saw that assistance wasn't on the racer's mind. He was heading straight for Frank, fists clenched. Frank gave Joe a quick nod and went into action.

"Nooooo! Joe, how could this have happened?" Frank wailed, playing the grief-stricken brother to the max.

Joe smiled up at his brother and shook his head at Frank's hammy acting. Then he began using his hands and feet to search for ways off the ledge. Suddenly Joe heard Moreno's voice shouting across the distance.

"You guys couldn't leave it alone! Well, I got rid of one Hardy pest. Time to exterminate the other."

"You'll never get away with it," Joe heard Frank shoot back.

"Want to bet?" Moreno taunted. "Heller and Alexander were too far back to see me take this shortcut. And you two are the only ones who would suspect I caused the landslide."

"And what about when we never show up?" Frank demanded. Joe could tell his brother was walking backward, leading Moreno past the ledge.

"Accidents happen all the time," Joe heard Moreno boast. "Everyone knows you two guys are amateurs. Or should I say *were*." Joe heard Moreno let out a whoop, and then he heard the sounds of blows. He tried desperately to hurry along, but he knew all too well how easily the ground could crumble beneath him. Every muscle rippled as Joe clung to the mountainside, straining to reach the top. Finally his hand reached up and he grabbed a fistful of air. He'd done it! With every last ounce of strength he could summon, he dragged himself up and over the side.

A few yards away he saw Frank fending off Moreno's punches, getting in a few of his own. But to Joe's experienced eye he could tell his brother wasn't up to his usual abilities. The hard ride had taken its toll. As Joe had hoped, Moreno's back was to him. Joe rose to his feet as quietly as he could. He sneaked up behind his brother's assailant and then, with an earsplitting cry, delivered a swift karate blow to Moreno's neck. The racer crumbled in a heap at Frank's feet.

"Gee, Joe," Frank joked. "Two against one? That's not very fair."

Joe smiled back at his panting brother. "Let's just say that this time we played by *his* rules."

Two hours later, Frank and Joe led a sullen Mauro Moreno into Julia Alvarado's office. Brett and Mike Baldwin were already there along with Carly and Chet. Don Jackson was there, too, since word had spread about what had happened on the cross-country trail. Frank and Joe had hiked out of the mountains with Moreno, and they had found a phone on the highway and called Alvarado, who sent a ride over to pick them up. Now, Julia sat with a serious look on her face, staring at Moreno.

149

"So," she said, tapping a pencil on her desk top. "We're all waiting. Would you care to explain yourself?"

Moreno confessed to his acts of sabotage one by one. It was he who had switched the trail marker and cut his own towrope in the waterskiing accident. "I hid a knife from the barbecue in my swimming trunks to do it."

"Why would you cause a water accident if you can't swim?" Joe asked, incredulous.

Moreno snarled his response. "Acting is another one of my amazing talents," he said.

Joe shook his head in disbelief.

"So you were the one who hid that stuff in Rich's toilet," Frank pressed.

Moreno sighed and then nodded glumly. "I needed to hide the stuff somewhere. And I figured if you guys really were detectives, it would make him look suspicious." He paused, looked down at his hands, and admitted, "I went after Joe with the snowplow, too. I wanted to give you a good scare just in case you were on my trail."

Don Jackson's face had turned bright red, and he practically sputtered when he finally spoke. "I can't believe what I'm hearing. You could have won fair and square. Why did you feel you had to cheat and lie and trick everyone? Someone could have gotten hurt."

"My sentiments exactly," Alvarado said, her mouth set in determination. "Because of that, I'm turning this case over to the police. What you've done could attract all sorts of negative attention to the sport, Mauro. You've set a terrible example for everyone, and I hope you realize it."

"What about Trace?" Joe wanted to know. "How much did he know about all this?"

"Nothing," Moreno insisted. "But if he found out anything, I figured he wouldn't snitch on me. When I went off trail, he was too far behind to see me."

"But we saw you," Frank said. "And you thought you could just get rid of us!"

"Sounds like you weren't thinking very clearly at that point," Jackson said. The man was obviously exasperated with his racer and amazed at what Moreno had done. "You can be sure your career is over."

Moreno sat in silence. He didn't even try being his usual arrogant self, Frank noticed.

"Good thing," Joe whispered to his brother. "Guys like him give sports a bad name."

Out in the winner's circle half an hour later, an official put a wreath around Rich Alexander's neck. In the last moments of the downhill, Alexander had pulled ahead of Trace Heller and had taken the championship. Now, Justine Kaplan was giving her racer a congratulatory hug, and the news media were champing at the bit to get their interviews with Alexander.

"I can't believe Moreno went to such lengths to get back at Alexander," said Joe.

"It was revenge. Revenge and desperation. He

couldn't risk losing," Frank pointed out. "He wanted us to suspect Alexander, and we did. Moreno was trying to railroad the guy."

"More like derail," said Joe.

Mike, Brett, and Carly started laughing. "Pretty good bad joke," said Brett. "Maybe you could have a career in comedy."

"Well, I know one thing," said Joe. "It's not in mountain biking."

"Why not?" Mike Baldwin asked.

"Too much work," Joe said.

Frank agreed. "I think we'll stick to being detectives for now," he said.

"And just race for fun," Chet offered.

Brett hugged Carly to him and smiled. "Guys, haven't you noticed? That's what mountain biking's all about!"

YOU COULD WIN A TRIP
TO THE PARAMOUNT THEME PARK
OF YOUR CHOICE

One First Prize: Trip for three to the Paramount theme park of the winner's choice.

Four Second Prizes: Four Single-Day Admission Tickets to the Paramount Park near you.

Twenty-Five Third Prizes: One Nancy Drew Mysteries Boxed Set and One Hardy Boys Mysteries Boxed Set.

Name_____Birthdate_____

Address_____

City_____State_____Zip_____

Phone_____

POCKET BOOKS/"Win a Trip to the Paramount Theme Park of Your Choice" SWEEPSTAKES
Official Rules: